D0031374

Praise for *The Samurai of Seville*

"This novel invites us to recover our history and colors the light of literary fiction."

—Kazuhiko Koshikawa,
former Japanese ambassador to Spain

"The stories that intertwine historical facts with adventure (sometimes with crime too) are normally excellent ones. *The Samurai of Seville* by John J. Healey is a clear example. Healey narrates with great care the episodes of a story that is also a romantic melodrama. The reminiscence of the traditional society and that of the old Seville, with the nobility, the villains and the passionate dames is very well described and Healey pulls it off. You just want to read it in one sitting thanks to the great rhythm and the emotions, together with the agile plot."

—*El País*

"Using a lean, concise narrative style . . . this story presents an absorbing view of the society of 17th-century Spain through a number of characters' perspectives, conveying the spirit of the land and the essence of each vivid character enmeshed within a larger web of relationships and interests."

—*Historical Novel Society*

"An exciting summer read. . . . At the center of this novel are love relationships, betrayals, friendships and the appreciation of Japanese and Spanish civilizations of the early 17th century. The best and worst features of these two ancient worlds are illuminated and brought together by the advent of necessity and greater glory."

—*Berkshire Eagle*

"A nice jumping-off point for new readers of historical fiction."
—*Library Journal*

"The undercurrent of melancholy that permeates the novel does not derive from the author's research but rather from his own life experience. He knows that in every coming and going there is a mixture of expectation and heartbreak, and there will arrive—on one side or the other—a point and time from which there is no return."
—Antonio Muñoz Molina,
author of *Separahad*

"Healey has created a narrative wonder mixing fictional and historical characters deeply immersed in the early years of the 17th century when Tokugawa Japan joined hands with the Spain of Philip III.... Healey offers an attractive, succinct text told with singular narrative skill. It reads effortlessly. Its immediacy and flow is absolutely cinematic."
—Prof. Juan Manuel Suárez Japón
(direct descendant of one of the Samurais
who went to Spain in 1613)

"Around this gentle love story, Healey coveys the way in which two very different cultures seek to honor and understand each other."
—*theidlewoman.net*

THE SAMURAI'S DAUGHTER

Additional Works by John J. Healey

Emily and Herman
The Samurai of Seville

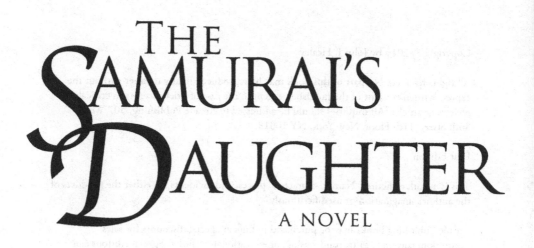

THE
SAMURAI'S
DAUGHTER

A NOVEL

JOHN J. HEALEY

Arcade Publishing · New York

First Edition

This is a work of fiction. Names, characters, places, and incidents are either the products of the author's imagination or used fictitiously.

Arcade Publishing books may be purchased in bulk at special discounts for sales promotion, corporate gifts, fund-raising, or educational purposes. Special editions can also be created to specifications. For details, contact the Special Sales Department, Arcade Publishing, 307 West 36th Street, 11th Floor, New York, NY 10018 or arcade@skyhorsepublishing.com.

Arcade Publishing® is a registered trademark of Skyhorse Publishing, Inc.®, a Delaware corporation.

Visit our website at www.arcadepub.com.

10 9 8 7 6 5 4 3 2 1

Library of Congress Cataloging-in-Publication Data
Names: Healey, John J., author.
Title: The Samurai's daughter : a novel / by John J. Healey.
Description: First Edition. | New York : Arcade Publishing, [2019]
Identifiers: LCCN 2019016173 (print) | LCCN 2019016819 (ebook) | ISBN 9781948924313 (ebook) | ISBN 9781948924306 (hardcover : alk. paper)
Subjects: | GSAFD: Historical fiction
Classification: LCC PS3608.E2355 (ebook) | LCC PS3608.E2355 S26 2019 (print) | DDC 813/.6—dc23
LC record available at https://lccn.loc.gov/2019016173

Jacket design by Erin Seaward Hiatt
Jacket illustration: iStockphoto

Printed in the United States of America

Translator's Introduction

The extraordinary manuscript that follows was discovered last year during renovations on the top floor of the palazzo Ca' da Mosto, the oldest in Venice. Written on parchment and bound in leather, the artifact has been thoroughly tested and authenticated. The final page, signed by the author, is dated in the year 1645 CE. The text is a memoir, ostensibly penned by a woman born in Spain in 1618. Her father was a Japanese samurai and member of the esteemed Date clan of Northern Japan. Her mother was a young noblewoman from the illustrious Medinaceli family of Soria, Guadalajara, and Seville, Spain. Apart from the numerous travels and adventures depicted, the memoir largely concerns the relationship between the author and her father, who arrived in Spain in 1614, as part of the first Japanese delegation to visit Europe.

The delegation consisted of twenty-two samurai warriors, a few Spanish naval officials, a Spanish priest, and numerous Japanese tradesmen. It left Japan in 1613 and reached southern Spain a year later. The idea, formed during the first years of the Edo period (1603–1868), was to speak directly with King Philip III of Spain and with Pope Paul V to try to establish trade with the territories of New Spain. In exchange, the Japanese were willing to admit additional missionaries into their kingdom. Though the Japanese emissaries were greeted in Madrid and in Rome with pomp and circumstance, the mission was a failure. Due to a conflagration that took place in Osaka during the delegation's absence, the shogun decided to ban all Christians from Japan, without exception. The delegation began their return journey in 1616. Six of the samurai warriors remained in Spain, settling in a small fishing village south of Seville, Coria del Río. Their descendants live and prosper there to this day. A seventh samurai, known simply as Shiro, became romantically involved with a Medinaceli heiress, who died giving birth to the author of this memoir.

Dedicato alla mia prozia, Soledad

"There is nothing, other than the present moment."
—*The Book of the Samurai* (*Hagakure*)
Tsunetomo Yamamoto

". . . my lord, you have begot me,
bred me, lov'd me . . ."

—Cordelia, *King Lear*
William Shakespeare

LIST OF MAIN CHARACTERS

THE DATE FAMILY:

Shiro, a samurai and the illegitimate son of a close advisor to Date Masamune, Katakura Kojuro, and Mizuki, Date Masamune's only sister.

Date Masamune, the fierce and wealthy, one-eyed, high lord and daimyo of Sendai, Japan, the city he founded; builder of Sendai Castle; and key councilor to the shogun. He is Shiro's uncle and protector.

Megohime Masamune, called Megohime. Date Masamune's wife.

Date Tadamune, Date Masamune's oldest son.

Mizuki, Shiro's mother and Date Masamune's only sister; a great beauty who first married a samurai warrior who was killed in battle before beginning an affair with Katakura Kojuro.

Soledad María Masako Date Benavides y de la Cerda, called Soledad María or Masako. She is the young woman who narrates this book, the daughter of Shiro and Guada.

THE MEDINACELI FAMILY:

María Luisa Benavides Fernández de Córdoba y de la Cerda, called Guada, the only daughter of Don Rodrigo and Doña Inmaculada. She married Julian of Denia, had a child with him—Rodriguito—after being raped by him. She subsequently had a grand love affair with Shiro the samurai and died giving birth to Soledad María Masako.

Soledad Medina y Pérez de Guzmán de la Cerda, called Doña Soledad Medina. The matriarch and wealthiest member of the family, Guada's aunt and protector, Soledad María Masako's great-aunt.

Carlos Bernal Fernández de Córdoba y de la Cerda, called Carlos. Guada's older brother and Soledad María Masako's uncle.

Rodrigo de la Cerda y Dávila, called Don Rodrigo. Guada and Carlos' father.

María Inmaculada Benavides Spínola, called Doña Inmaculada. Guada and Carlos' mother. She and her husband are also related to Doña Soledad Medina.

THE MEDINA SIDONIA FAMILY:

Rosario Martínez Gonzalez de Pérez de Gúzman, called Rosario. She is the last wife of Alonso Pérez de Gúzman, Seventh Duke of Medina Sidonia, a simple village girl the elderly duke fell in love with shortly before his death.

Francisco Alonso Pérez de Gúzman Conde de Bolonia, called Francisco. He is the son of Rosario and Alonso Pérez de Gúzman, Seventh Duke of Medina Sidonia.

THE O'SHEA FAMILY:

Charlotte O'Shea, called Charlotte. Born in Galway, Ireland to a successful whiskey trader with business in Spain.

Patrick Shiro Date O'Shea, called Patrick. Charlotte and Shiro's son.

María Carlota Fernández de Córdoba y de la Cerda y O'Shea, called Carlota. She is the daughter of Charlotte and Carlos.

THE SAMURAI'S DAUGHTER

– PART ONE –

– PART ONE –

I never knew my mother. When I imagine my birth, I see my wrinkly flesh covered in slime. I sense the ebbing darkness of dawn, and the sobbing of my great-aunt. I hear the wailing of the midwife, and a priest's mumbled prayers. My father's stoic silence. I can sniff the metallic scent of my mother's blood. My tiny ears register her last breath as a gravelly whisper. Our massive Moratalla estate surrounds us. The mansion and the gardens. The pebbled paths. The statues of Roman gods. The edges of the lawns sprinkled with orange blossoms. The Guadalquivir flowing beyond the gates.

The first two years of my life were lived between the Moratalla estate and my great-aunt's palace in Sevilla. Two years during which my father tried to recover from his loss, and for him to decide what to do with me. My great-aunt, Doña Soledad Medina, a noblewoman of great means, wished for me to stay with her, to grow up under her protection, to take my place in Sevilla society and be received at court in Madrid. But Father was a samurai, a princely member of the powerful Date clan that ruled the north of Japan. Years before, he had sworn allegiance to his uncle, the one-eyed warlord Date Masamune, and felt obliged to return. Despite Doña Soledad's protests, he refused to leave me behind. After much discussion and many tears, he promised her that when I attained the age of reason, he would bring me to Spain again, so that I might decide to which culture I wished to belong.

And thus it came to pass that in the spring of 1620, our ship set sail from Sanlúcar de Barrameda, the same port where Father and his samurai brethren had arrived six years earlier. He held me in his arms, waving my little hand in farewell to my great-aunt. She stood immobile on the wharf, dressed in black, flanked by her blue and gold carriage and her liveried coachmen. Father wore his finest samurai robe. The rigid hilts of his long and short swords pushed against my limbs. I was swathed in one of my mother's shawls. Gulls circled overhead. Everything was bathed in Andalusian afternoon light as the sails billowed and the ship came about into the currents of the estuary.

There were many passengers on board. Some were bound for Africa. Most were headed to the Spanish colonies in the New World. The voyage was unfolding smoothly until pirates appeared. Their captain was an Englishman who lived in Venice. He and his crew worked for a sultan that ruled Algiers. They piled aboard like ravenous beasts. Father swung his sword, protecting me, until they subdued him, beat him, and bound him. Another passenger, Caitríona, exquisite and barely fifteen, was grabbed by the captain and forced to watch as her Irish father was run through with an English cutlass. In dreams sometimes I hear her screams, along with the cheering of the men at the sight of the women being herded on deck to be abused for sport. All of them, including Caitríona's mother, were roped together to be sold as slaves.

I have been told that Caitríona was sent to the captain's cabin, holding me in her arms. He came down behind us, drunk and unwashed. He tried to force himself on her but was incapable. Livid with frustration, he began to slap her. He threatened to kill her. She swore to the heavens that she would never reveal his impotence and begged him to allow her to take care of me in his household. Then another ship arrived, and it distracted him. A representative of the sultan came on board, paid for the women, and bought Father as well, to use him as a warrior in some hellish arena. As Father was being shoved onto the other ship, he looked at the pirate captain and swore vengeance. The captain laughed and bellowed, "If you survive, and you won't, come to Venice to mete it out."

Caitríona and I were left in peace for the rest of the voyage. We arrived in Venice some days later. I retain glimmerings from the year we spent there. There was the captain's barren mistress, Maria Elena, in her gloomy palace. She clasped me to her breast, willing to excuse the captain's many vices for the enormity of the gift. There was a sour smell coming off the canal along the Giudecca, and the tolling bells of the Chiesa del Santissimo Redentore. I have vague memories of baths with Caitríona, surrounded by chatty maids. Our new clothes. The food and the feather beds. Maria Elena spoiled me. Caitríona never left me. A little dog slept next to me.

– II –

Father was put in an Algerian prison. They kept him in the same cell where, years before, the Spanish writer Cervantes had languished. With summer their games began, a vestige of the Roman conquest from centuries ago. Slaves and prisoners fought to the death against seasoned soldiers looking to impress their lords. The bloodthirsty public were frenzied bettors. Father made money for his captor, and during the first week the crowd would often turn against him, outraged that a foreigner could humiliate and murder so many soldiers of their faith. Rules were bent to his disadvantage. He was pitted against pairs of professional killers, and once he confronted a trio. But on each occasion, he prevailed, and following his warrior's code, he would bow to the remains of the men in a manner that even the least educated brute could see was genuine.

Then they unleashed beasts against him. An old bear, huge, disoriented, and fixed with a metal burr to make it angry. The cruelty of it caused Father to despise those who thought so little of such a noble creature. He gave it a death so swift it was painless. On the following day two razorback gorillas entered the ring. One of them succeeded in grabbing Father and hurling him to the ground. It knocked the wind from him. Wild cheers rose up from the amphitheater. But their massive heads soon rolled, infuriating their owner, and goading the crowds into louder cheering still. Father said he had never seen such creatures, and upon examining their corpses, he found them virtually human.

On the last day a woman charged with adultery was tied to a post with only Father to save her from three starved lions. Though he suffered a claw wound on his back that bled profusely, he killed all three before a multitude insane with excitement. He had been led to believe a victory would secure the woman a pardon, but on the following morning he was forced to witness her death by stoning. This so enraged him that en route back to the prison, he subdued his jailers, stole a skiff, and sailed for two days across the Mediterranean. Almost dead from thirst, he landed in Sicily near Akragas, and from there made his way north.

In Rome, he sought out Galileo Galilei, the scientist he had befriended on a former trip. Galileo took him in, fed him, and listened to all that had happened since they had last been together. He was appalled to learn what the pirates had done, and eager to help Father recover me. He provided Father with funds, a tailor to mend his garments and to make him new ones. A letter of introduction was written to a valuable contact in Venice, a man named Paolo Sarpi, an esteemed cleric and lawyer who, like Galileo, had run afoul of the pope and barely escaped with his life because of it.

In early autumn, Father arrived in the Serenissima Repubblica di Venezia. Paolo Sarpi took him in. They played chess together, and Sarpi learned about the pirate's whereabouts. Well-known and respected in the city, Sarpi got himself invited to the masked ball that Maria Elena held each year, and handed the invitation to Father.

Since no one in Venice knew what a samurai was, Father attended the ball as himself. His *kamishimo* outer jacket magnified the breadth of his shoulders. His weapons were polished to a blinding shine. His hair was pulled back and held in a black bow. His outer robe was black as well with gold threads that depicted the symbols of Date Masamune's household—the castle at Sendai, a sword, a rising crane. The only Venetian elements in his attire were a pair of velvet slippers and a black velvet mask, of the Arlecchino type, with a

5

devil's bump. He traversed the canal in a *sàndolo da barcariòl* steered by one of Paolo Sarpi's boatmen.

Revelers crowded the upper terrace, an expansive veranda overlooking the canal. Torches lit the corners, and as the guests arrived, a small orchestra played gentle airs by Gioseffo Zarlino and Giovanni Croce. Father said that as his boat approached, the mansion was lit like a temple, and his heart quickened. Later in my youth, I would make him repeat the thoughts that went through his mind at that moment. The moment when he realized that his child was inside, the flesh of his flesh, the little girl in whose veins coursed blood from samurai warlords and Spanish kings. He reminded himself that he had killed more than thirty men to get there, and that he was prepared to kill sixty more to rescue me.

Caitríona remembers how his costume drew admiring stares, especially from the signorinas who whispered to each other in wonderment about the identity of the stranger. Rich of pocket but *povere* in imagination, many of the young ladies had come arrayed as princesses, which they thought themselves to be. Their gowns were sewn from thick silks, forest green and plum, two of them a fiery red. Their powdered and cushioned alabaster bosoms rose and fell for all to savor. Seams festooned with lace or tiny pearls caught the torch and candle glow. Masses of hair were piled high, and feathered Colombina masks were held in place with gloved hands, masks that resembled birds from the tropics, birds from the salt marshes of the Laguna, birds of prey. The gentlemen strutted about with roosterish self-regard, in satin pantaloons and tricorn hats, excited by their exaggerated, protruding Bauta and Zanni masks that were fashioned as an homage to male tumescence. Many of the jackets and capes parodied military themes. Caitríona recalled one man had come as Caesar, another with spindly legs under a scandalously short skirt, as Alexander the Great.

As night wore on and the wine flowed, women danced with women, men with men, wives with other women's husbands. Father abstained. When approached and queried by sundry groups of the bold and curious, including Maria Elena herself, he simply said he was a guest of Paolo Sarpi. Given the latter's continuing aura of controversy with the Church, his renowned intellect and unswerving allegiance to the city, this reply only inflamed the allure of the stranger in their midst. That he was a foreigner could be easily ascertained from his accent, "but from where?" they asked him. "From far away," was all he deigned to say.

He found us in a drawing room, the one with walls covered with pink silk and lit by golden sconces. Caitríona and I were dressed as angels. We wore white diaphanous togas and, affixed with crisscross straps, elaborate feathery wings. We were sitting next to Maria Elena's mother, whom Caitríona remembers as elegant and severe, an elderly woman impervious to the evening's foolery. Father walked up to us, his mask still in place. Assuming a deficiency in English on the Italian woman's part, he bowed and addressed Caitríona in her native tongue.

"We have met before," he said.

"I would not know," she answered, imagining him to be one of Maria Elena's louche friends. "Your face is hidden."

"With good reason," he replied. "Do not be alarmed by what I am about to tell you. Do not allow the smile on your lips to flee."

"Why would I, sir?"

"We met at sea."

"At sea."

"Here now," said the dowager in Italian. "I'll have no more of this banter in so rude a tongue with this young lady."

I gazed up at him, intrigued by his mask. I'm told I even reached out to try and touch it.

"What is the woman saying?" Father asked Caitríona.

"That it is unbecoming to speak to me in a language she does not understand."

He turned to the older woman and tried some Spanish. "Pardon me, madam. My Italian is not what it should be. Perhaps you can understand me now."

"I do," she said, bowing her head.

"I do too," Caitríona said, still reeling from what Father had just revealed to her.

"And how is that?" he asked her.

"My family come from Galway, in Ireland. My father had much trade with Spain."

"In fact, you boarded the ship in Spain, no?" he said to her in Spanish.

Her smile faltered.

"What ship is this?" the old woman asked, opening a fan with which to cool herself.

It was at this point that I began to pluck at the feathers of Caitríona's wings.

"Stop that at once, young lady," said the dowager, pulling my hand away.

"A ship the English pirate attacked and plundered," Father said to the woman. "Killing this young woman's father, selling her mother into slavery, kidnapping her and this child of mine in a manner most foul."

Caitríona began to cry, silently, as she stared into his eyes with a look of panic and pleading. The older woman looked at him as if he were mad.

"Who are you, sir? How have you gained entry to this house? What manner of lies and libel are these you spew upon us?"

Once again, I began to pick at Caitríona's wings. This time, angry and distraught, the elderly woman closed her fan and slapped my wrist with it. I looked at the welt forming and began to cry. Father grabbed the fan from the woman's hand. She tried to get it back, unsuccessfully. People nearby began to stare.

"Try such a thing again, madam," he said, "and I shall sever that hand and throw it in the punch."

"This is outrageous!" she said, reverting back into Italian.

Father proffered an arm to Caitríona. "Shall I escort you and Soledad away from here?"

She told me she hesitated for the briefest moment before entrusting her fate to him, standing and taking me into her arms.

"This way," she said.

As the old woman stood, and staggered, and looked as if to faint, the nearest guests rushed to her aid. Father, Caitríona, and I made our escape down two flights of dark stairs reserved for the transit of servants. Word rippled through the various salons before reaching Maria Elena's ear as she danced on the veranda. Her screams stopped the orchestra. The pirate captain was playing cards with some of his men on a lower floor, but he surely heard the ruckus, for by the time we reached the pier and were stepping into the *sàndolo da barcariòl*, he and his men were after us. The drunken knave cocked a pistol and took aim, but with the wine in his blood, his agitation, and his dwindling eyesight, the shot missed its target and wounded Paolo Sarpi's boatman. Though the pirate captain and his drunken men then ran onto the pier, none of them possessed another firearm, and the boat slipped away. It was at that moment that Father saw a dagger in Caitríona's hand, a stiletto she'd stolen from the house soon after we first arrived, that she'd kept hidden all those months. He took it from her and threw it at the captain with great force. It pierced the pirate's throat, and he tumbled into the water. Caitríona confessed she watched him drown with great satisfaction.

The plan was to hide us in the Jewish quarter for a few days, an area locked off from the rest, but because of the wounded boatman we returned to Paolo Sarpi's home. He and his servants attended to the boatman, and Father apologized for implicating the noble Venetian in the evening's drama. Sarpi was nonchalant.

"I made provisions for this, just in case, and have a ship waiting. My personal effects are already on board. Come," he said, patting Father on the shoulder, "we've not a moment to lose."

The bandaged boatman was invited to join us, and we boarded a *caorlina* and were rowed to a ship moored off the Lido. By the time the pirate's men arrived at Paolo Sarpi's, along with sundry guests from the ball and a hastily gathered band of appointed authorities wielding torches and a writ of arrest, our ship had sailed.

– III –

We went south, heading for Brindisi. While Caitríona slept, Father held my hand and once again begged Paolo Sarpi's forgiveness.

"I cannot allow you to apologize any further," the Venetian said. "I have the pleasure one derives from doing a good deed. The drama and sudden change of place, this voyage, this morning sun and sea air, the prospect of staying with friends in Sicily, all of it is most stimulating. I feel alive for the first time in many months."

"You are kind to frame the events in such a fashion," Father said.

"It is the simple truth. And upon my return to Venice, I can assure you, my innocence shall be declared."

"Might you take the girl with you to Sicily?" Father asked, referring to Caitríona, for it was weighing upon him. "We cannot leave her alone," he said, "and I am going far away from any part of the world she is used to."

Sarpi placed a hand on Father's shoulder.

"My advice is that the three of you accompany me to Sicily. Its culture is deep, its inhabitants amusing, and it is part of the realm ruled by your patron, the king of Spain. From there you can return to Seville at your leisure, a lesson learned, where you and your child have a life of good fortune, and from where the young woman can make her way home to Ireland."

***

Father later told me he had thought of little else since our escape from Venice. The temptation to abandon the journey to Japan was strong. To insist on taking me there, after all we had been through, was surely an act of madness. If so much woe and calamity had come our way only a few days out of Sanlúcar de Barrameda, what might await us with half the world still left to cross? In Spain we had station, luxury, and a prestigious relative eager to spoil us. He remembered that when my mother, his beloved Guada, was in the last month of her pregnancy, she expressed interest in knowing Japan. He warned her that the journey was not worth the risk to women and children. But he was a stubborn man, and he had promised his mother—and his lord, Date Masamune—that he would return.

The new day passed. Night fell. The lights of Brindisi flickered in the distance. Mediterranean air filled the sails. The sea was calm. Our spirits were soothed by the steady, gentle noise the heavy hull made as it cut through the water. Paolo Sarpi sat aft sharing a meal with his servants. The crew went about their tasks, at ease and eager to reach port. From Brindisi, Paolo Sarpi would leave on another vessel for Sicily. Father and I would head east, toward Greece and the Ottoman Empire.

Before we landed, Caitríona spoke with Father. She held me, half asleep in her arms, and stood next him. "Don Shiro," she said. "I do not wish to go to Sicily. I wish to stay with you."

"You say this now," he replied, "ignorant of the thousands of leagues between here and my country."

"Even so," she said, staring at his hand that held on to some of the rigging. She told me years later it was the first time she noticed the scars about his joints.

"Signor Sarpi is a trustworthy and honorable man," Father said. "And he will do all he can to provide for you until you find your way home."

"I no longer have a home," she said.

"Is not Ireland the place you come from?"

"My father traded in whiskey," she said, "and made a good living from it. But his sons, my elder brothers, left him and started their own business trading in slaves. They earned twice the fortune my father had, in half the time, and made fun of him for his old-fashioned ways. After two years of decline, he gave in to their entreaties and agreed to join them. We were on our way to a slave market in Africa when the ship was attacked. I cannot help but think his death and my mother's fate were punishments from God. Now my family, my home in Galway, consists of my brothers and their kin, who I never wish to lay eyes on again."

Father listened and did not speak right away. Then he said, "I could make arrangements for you to stay at one of our homes in Spain. Soledad's great-aunt, after whom she is named, would do all that I ask, most especially in light of how well you have taken care of her grandniece."

"I wish to take care of her still," Caitríona said. "I have grown attached to her, and she saved my life."

"How so?"

"You must certainly suspect what the pirate's plans were for me—to take advantage of me in a fashion most gross before selling me off to the highest bidder."

"There is no need for you to revisit your entrapment by that man."

"It is my wish to," she said, "if only so that you might know what transpired. He was unable to do anything to me. Something you said to him as you were put on board the other ship with my mother bewitched him, or so he said. He made me swear not to say anything to his crew about it, and I told him I would agree if he allowed me to take care of the child, and to serve in his household. I believe he saw the advantages for him, and that is what he did. He knew it would please the woman he lived with there. Had Soledad not been born, had she not been there that terrible day, he would have killed me or sold me off without a second thought."

"If you stay with us," Father said, "it will be dangerous. Your life may be threatened again."

"I feel safe with you."

"My country, if we ever get there, will be most strange and foreign to you."

"I wish to know it in your company."

And thus it was decided that Paolo Sarpi would travel to Sicily alone. Caitríona O'Shea would accompany Father and me to the Orient.

***

A farewell dinner was celebrated before each party went on its way. Caitríona described large bowls of pasta flavored with garlic, olive oil, and parsley. Then came platters of fish grilled with tomatoes and fennel. Sarpi ordered the best wine, a deep red from Catania that tasted, she said, of slate and cherry. It had been harvested and pressed from grapes planted by the Romans.

"May God bless you," Sarpi said, standing and raising his cup.

"And may the devil keep you," Caitríona replied with the Galway lilt in her voice.

"May each of you live the life you desire," Father said with a serious look and tone that gave the merry group pause.

After Caitríona and I retired, Paolo Sarpi invited Father to join him for a walk down by the harbor. Father said he would have preferred to turn in with us, but he was loath to refuse such a simple request from a man who had done so much for us. He said that Sarpi spoke with a slight stammer and was one of those erudite gentlemen prone to run on at great length and detail, incapable of abbreviating any tale or opinion.

That evening, the Venetian held forth on the evolution of Adriatic fishing practices and then recounted a story of how he had once convinced a German prince that pasta grew on trees, trees that only required scant irrigation, trees harvested twice a year using scythes. He was laughing so much while telling the tale it was hard for Father to understand him. He reviewed the lands and cultures we would be sailing by en route to Japan. As the man's faltering voice droned on, Father said his mind wandered. He breathed in the harbor smells rising up from the water, rising up from wooden piles driven into sand, dank and briny odors rising in the cool air. He said a new moon was in the sky that night and that with each passing minute more stars emerged.

"I have a colleague you might run into on your travels," Sarpi was saying.

"Who might that be?" Father asked.

"A wealthy Roman called Pietro Della Valle, a cultivated man gone off to explore many of the lands you shall visit. The last I knew of him he was ensconced somewhere in Persia."

They said goodnight standing at the entrance of the inn. Paolo Sarpi stepped forward as if to offer an embrace, but Father stood back and bowed three times instead. Sarpi smiled and did his best to return the gesture.

— IV —

The ship was to take us to Piraeus. From there we would find another to reach Tartus. From Tartus the plan was to cross overland to Basra or Qurain in the hope of finding passage to India and beyond. But as we approached Greece the sea turned gray and choppy. A mammoth storm gathered and fell upon us. The crew struggled to reach shore before succumbing to the fury of it. With the island of Paxos in sight, the sails ripped, the mast cracked and then split in two. A towering wave heaved the hull over on its side.

Of the few who knew how to swim, only Father survived. He gathered his weapons into a sack that he fastened about his neck. Once in the water, Caitríona and I clung to him as he swam. Others around us paddled frantically, but he swam employing long, slow strokes until he found a section of the mast we held fast to. Night overtook us and hid a terrible tableau of drowning men and howling winds. The sea calmed at dawn, and in a driving rain we made our way onto a beach of smooth black pebbles.

We staggered ashore and got out of the rain, huddling under low cliffs of limestone. Father found a cave where we sat shivering and relieved. By noon the rains had ceased and the sun emerged. Dead sailors and some of the wreckage floated in the shallows. More concerned with finding food, Father left the bodies where they were and walked us inland. The island appeared to be large. Although there were no immediate signs of habitation, olive trees grew in abundance, grass grew in meadows crossed with streams, and there were goats for milk and meat.

We slept under the stars that first night wondering what would become of us.

"I warned you," Father said to Caitríona, "that if you stayed with me your life might once again be fraught with danger."

"And yet for being with you I have once again been saved."

The logic of her reasoning was lost on him.

"I have had my fill of the sea," he said. "To think of the distances I traveled from Sendai to Spain with barely an incident, and now I cannot set foot upon a ship without disaster striking."

Caitríona told me the only thing I said that day was "*Io voglio tornare a Venezia.*"

***

Father discovered an abandoned shepherd's hut above a protected cove. The cove had a curving beach and fine sand and the sea there was a clear turquoise. At the far end of it a fresh stream cascaded between boulders from above that you could stand under. He stabbed fish with his short sword that he tied to a whittled spear. In the late afternoons, he and Caitríona swam together and did their best to forget the horror of the wreck. During our first week there he considered pressing on, to try to discover who else might be on the island, to see if he could find someone to help us continue on our way. But he was exhausted from all that had happened since leaving Sanlúcar, and he decided it best to rest. It was during this time that Caitríona heard his story and mine.

He told her he was a samurai from Japan and he explained what that meant. He told her he was born out of wedlock and raised by his mother and her brother, Date Masamune, the most powerful daimyo of the north. How from a young age he had been curious about the outside world, how he learned English and Spanish, and how, when the shogun and Date Masamune organized an expedition to sail to Mexico and Spain, he was put on board to spy for them in order to ensure that, upon the delegation's return, its leader, Hasekura Tsunenaga, spoke the truth.

He told her about his year at sea, about Mexico and Cuba and his arrival in Sanlúcar de Barrameda, and how he caught the fancy of the elderly Duke of Medina-Sidonia because they shared an obsession with swords. He told her how he fell in love with my mother, the duke's niece, who was sixteen and already married to a nobleman who was mean and unfaithful to her. The Duke of Medina-Sidonia introduced Father to the king, Philip the Third, and he was well received. Of all the samurai he was the only one to embrace the Spanish culture. He told her how he defended my mother's honor and, with the king's approval, killed her husband in a sword fight, and how when the delegation from Japan left Spain to return home he stayed behind, disobeying his uncle's instructions because he wished to be with my mother. He spoke of how she died a year later when I was born, and how, in the end, he decided to return to Japan and bring me with him. He explained how my great-aunt, who was on in years, was so distraught at our leaving he felt obliged to promise her that when I reached the age of reason, he would do all he could to bring me to Spain again so that I might choose which of my two cultures to live in. He told her all of this in bits and pieces, and only because Caitríona was insistent in her questions.

We adapted to life on the island. The summer and early autumn were good to us. The days and nights blended into each other. Father taught me Japanese and Spanish, Caitríona taught me English. We slept next to each other in the shepherd's hut. One night, Caitríona changed places with me and clung to Father in the darkness.

Moonlight streamed in through an opening in the roof and I could see them kissing and touching each other.

Once I saw her naked on top of him near the beach, when they thought I was napping, and she was crying out, and I was angry with him for hurting her and ran to help her. That was when they told me they were happy together and that Caitríona was my new mother.

Looking back on the months we spent there I see it was an Eden. It was like the story in the Christian bible—Father, the first man; Caitríona, the first woman. There was no one else to chastise or censor them. His courtship of my mother had known long periods of frustration. It was riddled with delays and obstacles before they were allowed the peace of an embrace. Father and Caitríona had no courtship at all. They lay with each other whenever they wished. They were the world itself for a time, observed and mediated by no one but me.

She learned to respect the guilt that sometimes took hold of him. Recollections of my mother made him feel he was betraying her memory, and they reawakened his devotion to what had been their short-lived life together, a life that breathed on within my body. Caitríona made room for it, and he was aware of her graciousness and touched by it. I suspect that some of the passion he knew with my mother was fueled by difficulty and the force of sin. But with Caitríona, their passion rose up from the earth and the sea.

And it was there on that island, the very same one where Circe had captivated Ulysses, that I finally had the beginnings of a childhood. The loss we suffered in Spain, the violence of the pirates, the forced and cosseted luxuries of Venice, all of that faded under the cleansing sun in the transparent waters of Paxos. We drank from clean streams. We ate fish and goat. We dressed as we wished, if

19

at all. We rose with the sun and slept when night fell. I counted pebbles and shells, fruit bats and shooting stars. It was only when the rains came late in autumn that Father decided it was time to leave.

Caitríona suspected she was with child by then. Villagers on the northern end of the island took us to the mainland. From there we reached Piraeus and from Piraeus we boarded another ship bound for Alexandria. These voyages were calm and uneventful, and by the time we reached the ancient city of learning, its library long squandered, its lighthouse a ruin of stones, its populace pulverized by plague and decades of decline, our island idyll was behind us.

***

From Alexandria, we traveled to Cairo by mule. After a few days there, astonished by the pyramids, we found a way to push east. Caitríona's pregnancy was beginning to show by then. The journey by caravan across the desert to reach the port of Ain Al-Sukhna was wondrous. The blinding hot days, the cold nights, the acrid smell of the camels, their nasty tempers, the wise eyes of our Bedouin companions. We felt cleansed and calmed. We thrived on dates and figs. I learned to appreciate and measure the preciousness of water.

In Ain Al-Sukhna, we boarded a large dhow with bright white sails and made our way south on the Red Sea. Father was content. And being content made him nervous, for though he wished to believe the worst was behind us, he knew he must never let down his guard. There was a placid steadiness to our days aboard the dhow that mirrored the surrounding landscape and its inhabitants. The Nubian people living on the shore looked like a race of gods. The kindness and reserve of the Arabs who held the tiller and worked the rigging of the dhow were nothing like the noisy, rambunctious Venetians. Father looked at Caitríona and me. He smiled at us. He took my hand. It was as if he had regained a kingdom lost to him since my mother died.

I suppose such feelings of peace and redemption are necessary at times, even for a samurai warrior. Even though, for a price, the men sailing the dhow might have slit our throats. Even though sharp-toothed sea creatures pursued the hull, searching for prey. Even though life's squalid side would soon come roaring at us yet again.

Dear Paolo,

I hope this finds you well, and living in the manner I now wish to emulate after too many years of wandering and exploration. What drives people like myself to eschew the comforts of home by roaming so afar astray is a mystery. I have come to believe your way of life, dedicated to scholarship and contemplation, is far superior.

The tragic tale I am about to set down will serve to explain my knowledge of your whereabouts.

After much traveling and study of the cultures found in Persia, I took it upon myself to make a visit to the great Indian subcontinent before returning home. About two months ago my party and I arrived at the port of Aden, where all of the British East India Company ships stop for provisions to and from Surat. It was there I made the acquaintance of your friends—the most elegant and fierce gentleman from Japan known as Shiro, his small child, and a lovely Irish lass now in her fifth month of pregnancy. The Asian warrior recalled your having mentioned me to him and I was soon apprised of the adventures they survived in Venice thanks to your admirable intervention. How I wish I could report that what happened soon afterward had an outcome equally felicitous, but alas, I cannot.

The first ship to come along heading east was unusually small, the HMS Attendant, *of some one hundred tonnes. Its captain assured us that in* exchange for bearing up with what would be close quarters during the estimated three-week journey, we would arrive in Surat infinitely sooner than if we were to wait for the next, much larger vessel that was not due to arrive for at least another month. This being the case, and what with the engaging spirit of the captain and the youth of my new acquaintances, we agreed to book passage that day. I believe that as trade has grown and coffers swelled, more and more ships sail the route to and fro, and as the number of embarkations increase, the quality of the hired seamen diminishes proportionately.

Almost from the outset the captain's lack of authority and his crew's unhealthy disposition were apparent. The seamen were driven by envy and lust, and they displayed an astonishing aversion to cleanliness. They viewed the samurai with undiluted suspicion and made fun at his expense without any regard for rank, gallantry, or propriety. The only woman on board was the Irish lass, whom all of these lowly men began to covet in a most malevolent manner, allowing many vulgar comments to escape their lips, while miming obscene acts of lascivious aggression that left little to one's imagination.

It made all of us uncomfortable in the extreme, most especially the captain. One obstreperous individual was singled out for a flogging by the First Mate, in the hope it might persuade the brute's comrades to cease in their salacious behavior. But the punishment had quite the opposite effect, and begot a mutiny. A gang of them bludgeoned the First Mate to death. The captain, grabbing his charts, locked the gunroom and threw the key overboard. The crew, enraged and inflamed with a murderous fever, began to pull at the pregnant young woman's garments. A long boat was lowered and the captain and my party managed to get into it. The samurai, wielding two gleaming weapons, a long and a short sword, fought off the mob as best he could while insisting that the lass with

23

child join us in the long boat. But he was unable to pass his little girl to us.

The Irish lass, mad with grief, attempted to swim back to the ship. When we succeeded in apprehending her, she tried to drown herself. The captain was forced to tie her down. As we rowed away all we could see were the mob of ruffians, cutlasses and clubs in hand, closing in on the lone samurai and his child. You could not imagine a more horrific sight.

As the captain knew, and as we, to our great relief, soon discovered, the coast lay just over the horizon. We reached it safely and were taken in for the night by a family of fishermen. We then spent six weeks making our way to the coast of Syria from whence we sailed, arriving yesterday evening here in Trieste. The Irish lass has not spoken since our escape. I was entrusted by the samurai to bring her to you, an obligation I will gladly fulfill upon receiving your reply. She carries a letter from the Samurai and within her womb the samurai's child, now his only living survivor.

Your devoted friend,
Pietro Della Valle

– VI –

Caitríona later told me that all she could think about on the journey from the Orient to Sicily was that the nuns and the priests of her Galway childhood had been proven right. The magnitude of her sins, and the extravagance of the pleasure she derived from them, had not gone unnoticed, and they were being paid for in full. The horror of human life had been laid out for her. Hell had been revealed to her as something well attainable here on Earth. It suddenly made sense to her that the devil had once been a favored angel of God. For only a spirit so familiar with God's grace would know how to wreak the cruelest sort of pain and havoc upon a reckless sinner as inconsiderate of scripture as she.

Once Pietro Della Valle left Caitríona in Sicily, Paolo Sarpi devoted himself to her. He told her it was a fitting way for him to conclude his exile. He removed her from the bustle of Palermo and found them a villa in the hills near Carini that commanded a view to the sea, down past the ruins of the ancient Hyccara. It was at this property one autumn morning, seated on a terrace under a pergola adjacent to an olive grove, that he finally got her to speak.

In the midst of making conversation for the both of them, a methodology he had been using for some time, she—most unexpectedly—uttered a response. He closed his eyes as if to give thanks to the gods, but otherwise he made no special cause of it, so as not to risk herding her back to silence.

Wasps feeding on grapes dangling above them inspired a vacuous observation. "I hope they leave some for us," he had said, "for the grapes are at their ripest now and have a luscious look to them."

"That one's being eaten alive," was what she responded, with her head cast down, peering over the fullness of her abdomen.

He followed her gaze and came upon a wasp that had been injured in some manner, but it was still aquiver, and surrounded by a legion of ants feasting on it.

"I don't think it feels anything," he said. "I don't think it's in any pain."

"You do not know that for certain," she said, lifting her head and looking at him.

"No," he said. "You're right."

"They probably made it very painful for him," she said.

It was clear she was no longer thinking of the wasp.

"But now it is over and done," he said. "And he is at peace."

"What about the little girl?" she asked, tears forming in her eyes.

He leaned forward and placed a hand on her knee.

"You mustn't think about that," he said. "You'll have your own child soon and you must endeavor not to burden it with your sorrow."

She wept for a good hour after that, as he held her hand, and when she was done she stood and crushed all the ants under the soles of her sandals. That evening she ate with appetite while he told her of his plan to accompany her to Spain once the baby was born.

***

My half-brother came into the world at twilight in Caitríona's bedroom at the villa. The local midwife and the midwife's sister attended. She told me they were astonished to see that she seemed to enjoy the pain, the freedom it gave her to scream as loud as she wished. She knew Paolo Sarpi was listening below on the veranda overlooking the Mediterranean. She knew he would be agitated and appalled by the primitive reality of what was taking place upstairs, her agony piercing him like arrows. She said she was gripped by the thought that every person she knew, herself included, and every person she would ever know or see, came into the world in this manner. And she knew that, when combined with the primal nature of eating, defecating, copulating, and dying, the thoughts and theories, the books and paintings that Paolo Sarpi granted such importance to, fell by the wayside, unmasked as stratagems concocted to evade the fundamentals of human existence.

With each scream she saw the world more clearly, a bloody and raw place she had been pulled into, an abattoir of frenzied hunting and killing. Art and religion's decorative ramparts, the fine points of etiquette and clothing, were ill suited to compete with the digestive tracts and genital hungers of the creatures surrounding her.

She thought about her mother who had gone through this for her, who had suffered the drunken lusts and violent temperament of her father, her mother who had raised two ungrateful sons, who had started life as a carefree girl from Sligo, only to be condemned to live out her days being abused as a slave in some feudal, far-off land. She screamed for her mother. She screamed at her thick, redheaded brothers whose ugliness and villainy had brought such shame and violence upon her, her wealthy brothers who still lived in blissful ignorance of what they had done.

The Sicilian women hovered over her, touching her, placing their garlic-tinged fingers in her most intimate places, trying to assuage her, urge her on, praying for her while making comments so lewd— once they divined the sex of the emerging infant—it made her scream with laughter at times as well. She told me it was only after they had cut the cord and disposed of the afterbirth, after they had washed the child in tepid water steeped in chamomile, and cleaned her and placed the child with her, leaving her, going downstairs with their pails and bloodied linen to tell the signore—who they assumed to be the father despite the unusual shape of the baby's eyes—it was only then she permitted herself to think of Father.

It was not the first time he rescued her in Venice that came to mind, but rather the second time, the shipwreck off Paxos. She recalled what it had felt like to cling to him in the sea as the storm raged, holding onto me as he swam for the three of us, how he had found us food and shelter. She told me that as she held his baby boy against her breasts in that dark Sicilian villa, she went back, as she so often did, to the months they had shared together, living by the cove, where the baby had been made, where she'd known such desire, when sin had been a blessing.

– VII –

When mother and child were sufficiently recovered, Paolo Sarpi and Caitríona sailed from Palermo to Málaga. They arrived on a Sunday morning just after dawn. The water of the harbor was so clear she could see through it and watch the anchor biting the sand. A skiff rowed out to retrieve them and their effects. A carriage took them to breakfast at an inn, where later they boarded a coach bound for Córdoba. Two days later another coach brought them to Sevilla.

Both of them found southern Spain backward but charming, not unlike the Sicilian countryside they had come from. Caitríona thought that Sevilla looked to be as dirty as Palermo, but burdened with more formality, in dress and manners. The food was heavier, the wines too sweet. Plagued with fetid drainage, mosquitoes, and a large population of Catholic clergymen, Sevilla was cosmopolitan and colorful nevertheless. Once oriented, they were relieved to find the noble neighborhood, where enormous homes were built close to each other. These were the palace-like abodes that are so familiar to me now, with their well-guarded gates and tall white walls, their palm fronds and hanging bougainvillea.

They were admitted to the grandest of them all, the Casa de Pilatos, where my great-aunt lived. They were asked to wait in the main courtyard. They sat on one of the stone benches in the shade, facing a gurgling fountain, pomegranate and grapefruit trees, and a statue of Emperor Trajan. One of Doña Soledad's handmaidens appeared offering water.

In those days my great-aunt was confined to a sturdy chair that a crew of manservants moved her about in. She was recovering from a fall and pain was a constant companion. Though it tested her temper, she made a great effort to transcend the discomfort. She told me her handmaiden related to her why the visitors had come, and that the news filled her heart with agitation.

"How do they seem?" she asked the handmaiden.

"Señora?"

"Are they proper people? Are they properly dressed?"

"Yes, Señora."

"Do they seem genuinely foreign?"

"Yes, Señora. In fact, their Spanish is poor."

"How tiresome."

"They have an infant with them."

"An infant, you say?"

For a brief moment, flagrantly ignoring the time that had passed since my father's departure, she hoped against hope.

"Yes, Señora. A baby boy."

"Ah . . . Ask them to stay, and tell them I shall see them at supper. Show them to the Roman Suite and see they have all they require. And have Manolo prepare something tasty this evening."

It had been a long time since Soledad Medina had kept a houseguest, or entertained, and the prospect stimulated her, almost as much as the possibility of having some news of Father and me. In fact, she found herself incapable of waiting until the evening meal. After fifteen minutes of deliberation, she had herself carried to the Roman Suite. The men transporting the chair were ordered to leave the guest rooms immediately, for as they carried the elderly woman in, they encountered Caitríona feeding her baby. Caitríona apologized for not standing so that she might curtsy properly, but otherwise showed no embarrassment at having her breasts exposed.

The first thought entering my great-aunt's mind was that she had not seen a creature as young, charming, or beautiful since—in much happier times—my mother. Paolo Sarpi emerged from an adjacent room and introduced himself. Doña Soledad was surprised to see such an older man with the girl, but as a woman of the world she took it in stride, and recalled how her own Alonso Pérez de Guzmán, the late Duke of Medina-Sidonia, had fallen in love with a girl in his service easily forty years his junior. She addressed them in perfect Italian.

"I understand you bring news of my great-niece and of her father, the gentleman from Japan."

"We do, my lady," answered Caitríona.

"If you will permit me," Paolo Sarpi interjected, "I will happily offer our gracious hostess a full account of how it is that young Caitríona here has come to this noble house."

"By all means," said Caitríona, deferring to him.

He prefaced the tale with shameful assurances that Father and I were last seen in good health. These assurances caused Caitríona to blush and stare at the floor. Both gestures were duly noted by Soledad Medina. Then he related how our ship had been taken by pirates, only a few days after embarking from Spain. He told what he knew about Father's time in Algiers, and went into great detail describing the house and situation of Maria Elena in Venice. He placed emphasis on how much time and care Caitríona had devoted to my welfare. He omitted all mention of Father and Caitríona's subsequent journeys to Greece, to Egypt, and their failed attempt to reach India. He elected instead to tell another lie, one that mirrored the advice he had given Father in Brindisi, saying that Caitríona had come with him directly to Sicily.

"It was the samurai's most fervent wish," he concluded, "that Caitríona find some way of being of service to your ladyship, so that she might find a way for herself and her child to survive in this world."

Soledad Medina studied the scholar's face as he delivered his disquisition, looking for lapses in the story, or any signs of equivocation. She told me that though she felt stirrings of suspicion, they were still too vague in nature. It was then that the baby boy ceased suckling and turned his head in her direction. That the little fellow was part Japanese and directly related to me was immediately evident. Doña Soledad reached out and took the boy's tiny hand and kissed it.

"What have you named him?" she asked.

"Patrick, after a beloved uncle," she said. "Patrick Date O'Shea."

It made the older woman laugh.

"I see there are some details you've yet to mention," my great-aunt said to Paolo Sarpi, while looking into Caitríona's eyes. "You must rest. We can continue to get to know each other at supper."

Once their hostess had been carried from the room, Caitríona turned to Paolo.

"What possessed you to lie like that?"

"Instinct," he said. "The same instinct that told me to speak for you. I'm not at all certain this woman could survive knowledge of the events that still weigh on us. The samurai impressed upon me the degree of devotion she felt for her niece, and that she continues to feel for the little girl. Her main reason for living is to be here when the girl is returned to her. The truth would break her heart—and cloud any chance for your success. She might expire on the spot, or wash her hands of the whole business."

Though she understood his logic, Caitríona had her doubts. It pained her conscience to keep a horrible truth from a woman who had the look of someone well accustomed to surviving disappointment.

***

The evening meal began shortly after eleven, and took place in the salon dominated by a Giuseppe Recco still life. The marble dining table displayed a mosaic portrait of Mary Magdalene. Two young men dressed in daffodil-yellow livery came through the arabesque doorways and served grilled fish, along with a rice dish cooked with olives and honey. They served a chilled Manzanilla wine in crystal goblets.

"Might I presume you are not a married couple?" Doña Soledad asked the Venetian.

"You may."

"And might I be correct in assuming that Shiro the samurai is the father of your little Patrick?" she asked Caitríona.

"Yes, madam," Caitríona answered with a blush. Then she bit her lip and went on. "But I feel compelled to tell you the truth of how the relationship came about. It was I who approached him, I who sought his comfort, I who took the first steps. He saw my father murdered. He was taken away on the same ship as my mother. He escaped after unimaginable trials to come for his daughter and me. He saved my life, twice. I was alone in the world and never had I encountered such a gentleman. I was besotted. But all the time that I was fortunate enough to be with him, he never once lost sight of, or broke free from, the profound connection he had to your niece. Try as I did to distract him from it, he maintained an abiding love for Doña Guada."

Soledad Medina looked down at her plate.

"I promised the samurai I would escort the signorina here and see she was taken in and properly cared for," Paolo Sarpi said, hastening to put off any adverse conclusions on the part of their hostess.

But the hostess had been thinking of little else since that afternoon's first interview, and after careful consideration she had already arrived at a firm determination.

"Before they departed, I tried to convince Shiro to remain here," she said. "I offered him many advantages, offers that will still apply upon their return. One of the things I said to him was that for however difficult it might be for him to then imagine, it would only be natural that he find another companion someday to trust his heart to, and that when such an attachment occurred, I would welcome the both of them. Though half of Sevilla thinks me mad, I have willed the entirety of my estates and holdings to Shiro and Guada's little girl. That he has sent you to me, Caitríona, entrusted your welfare to me through the offices of this distinguished gentleman from Venice, assures me his affections toward you were not superficial, but solid—and you have borne him a son. You and your baby boy shall be safe with me. You will be *my* companion now, and we shall both wait and pray together for his safe return."

Caitríona was awash in tears at this point, tears of gratitude and tears of shame. It was then they heard the baby cry. Caitríona felt her milk gathering and excused herself.

"Let him sulk a while, child," Soledad said, bidding with her hand that the young woman remain seated. "Or you shall spoil him."

But Caitríona did not return to her seat. Drying her eyes with her napkin, she said, "Oh, but I mustn't, my lady. Please forgive me."

And with that she was gone.

"She is young still," Paolo Sarpi said.

"She is a mother," Doña Soledad replied. "I very much approve of her decision to ignore my attempt to maintain an absurd social decorum. My admonishment was but a test, in fact, and she has passed it glowingly. I, once upon a time, and my Guada, had she lived, would have done the same."

Tears came into Doña Soledad's eyes, which the Venetian misinterpreted.

"I would like to say, my lady, that your behavior in this entire matter is exemplary. It has far exceeded my expectations. Your generosity is an inspiration and—might I suppose—as unusual here in Sevilla as it would be among the nobility of Venice."

She waved his flattery away and took a long drink of wine.

"I have lived a long time, Signor Sarpi. Though I have been fortunate in that I have not had to witness such horrors as Signorina O'Shea has at such a young age, there is little, bad or good, I have not seen by now. I consider myself a keen judge of character, of people in general. It is a quality I had to learn from numerous mistakes made along the way. And so, though I am honored by the dignity and the strength of character you have demonstrated, fulfilling your promise to the samurai in such a selfless fashion, and though I have been truly moved by the degree of forthrightness Caitríona has shown in explaining herself to me—my instincts, my heart, my graying soul are certain you are hiding something."

Paolo Sarpi blanched with alarm.

"What, pray my lady, might you be referring to?"

"Come, Signor Sarpi, before the girl returns. Tell me the truth of how it came to be that she and her baby were separated from the samurai and my relation. I could not help but notice how she spoke of him in the past. Even if my heart shall be unable to bear it, tell me the truth."

Soledad Medina was devoted to my mother. It was a source of significant irritation for my mother's parents. In their opinion, it gave society the impression that the wealthy dowager cared more for their daughter than they had. They would often claim that, after all, it was they who conceived and raised my mother. It was they who procured an advantageous marriage for her. That the groom proved to be a cad was not their fault. That my mother got pregnant because her husband raped her was less important to them than the fact it produced a male heir—Rodriguito—a future nobleman and grandee of Spain, a child blessed with impeccable lineage who, since Mother's tragic demise, it had been their great pleasure to care for and educate within the walls of their palace and estates.

They were appalled by what my mother did afterward, that she fell in love with my father—a "heathen" from halfway around the world. Though they never met Father, they denied his so-called charm, his claims to royalty, and the favor he had gained in the eyes of the king. And then Mother made it worse by being happy with him, getting pregnant again, and then dying as she gave birth to me, a bastard baby girl. I believe that for quite some time they harbored the belief that Mother's death had been a just punishment for her sins.

And so it bothered them enormously when Doña Soledad Medina's surge of affection toward their daughter coincided precisely with her disgrace, the collapse of her marriage, and the consummation of her feelings for my father. Though she was too well mannered to say so, it was clear to them that Soledad Medina considered their feelings to be provincial, and that she had come to hold them in low esteem.

From the day my mother died, Doña Soledad dressed in black. A mass was celebrated every morning, to pray for my mother's soul and for my safe return. Before we left Spain, Doña Soledad signed over the entirety of her properties and her enormous fortune to me. It stung my mother's parents to the quick to know that their daughter's first child—a son, a Spaniard, the legitimate heir as far as they were concerned—had been ignored by their esteemed relative in favor of the illegitimate, half-breed baby girl that was me.

Soledad Medina's world had diminished with time, the fate of a woman blessed with longevity. Her men were dead: her unfaithful but not unamusing husband; her gallant lover, the Duke of Medina-Sidonia; and her two sons, once upon a time sweet little boys who in adolescence became crass, bulky, and insolent. Since the muted reaction of my mother's parents to their daughter's rape, Doña Soledad had pulled back from them. From the moment they took Mother's little boy, who they would make their heir, into their house, Soledad Medina made a point of seeing them as infrequently as possible. By taking my mother into her care, she relived her youth. Through Mother's romance with my father, she saw life once again as something vibrant and meaningful. Then, suddenly, Mother departed this earth, and the samurai took me away. It was my return that she lived for.

***

She told me about the day she fell and broke her hip. It was after mass at the chapel at her estate, La Moratalla. She was taking her customary walk through the formal gardens up to the Roman ruin where Mother's grave is. She slipped and fell backward. The pain surprised her as she lay in the grass looking at the sky through her veil. She said she thought at first that she might die, for she had the lucidity to recognize that under her luxurious skirts was an aging animal, and that this was how aging animals met their end—when their bones could no longer carry them. While her handmaiden ran off in search of the priest and the doctor, she recalled a day when she and my very pregnant mother, along with Father and Mother's first little boy, took a picnic to the river below. She recalled how happy they had been, how content she felt having us safe with her. She sat with my mother in the shade of a tree on the shore of the Guadalquivir, in a place where it narrowed and flowed cold and clean, and they watched my father teaching the little boy to swim. They'd been a family, she said, a family that was original and *simpática*, the sort of unexpected group her own liberal father would have loved, and that her dour mother would have been horrified by.

When the maid returned with the doctor and the obsequious priest who fell to his knees in prayer like a bad actor, and as the doctor prodded, as the other men with them lifted her onto a cot to carry her back to the mansion, she told me how she remembered other good times to keep the pain at bay. Most of all, she went back to an evening when she had walked through those same gardens many years earlier—while her husband was away with one of his lady friends. She had walked there with the Duke of Medina-Sidonia at her side. Her sons were still little and they ran on in front of them, conquering imaginary Moors with swords the duke had fashioned from sticks. She said, whispering it to me, that what she most remembered from that day was the moment the duke bade her pause, when he pressed her against the trunk of a tree and kissed her, moving his hands over her, the breathtaking thrill of it.

– PART TWO –

-PART TWO-

– IX –

Some years later, Father told me what happened aboard the ship on which the mutiny took place—the blood and the savagery—for I had blocked it from memory. The rage and then the horror that gripped the mob of men hell-bent on killing us. Rage flowed between them like a drug, but then the horror as they began to see their number diminish, as hands and arms littered the deck, as they slipped on their mates' blood and innards. I cowered behind Father, screaming as he went about his task like a dancer of death. When it was down to just one miserable man, the fellow dropped his sword and jumped overboard to drown.

Father suffered many bruises, but no gashes, punctures, or broken bones. He carried me to the other extreme of the ship, up the stairs onto the aft deck, and set me down by the helm. He spoke to me gently and sang softly to me until I stopped crying and fell into a deep slumber. He said it was only then that he allowed himself to rest, to lie back and stare at the sky. What he most remembered was how beautiful the clouds were, for it was early evening by then, and they had taken on brilliant tints of pink and orange as the sun began to dip below the horizon.

This was how the Dutchmen found us when their ship came alongside. They boarded armed with muskets. As they surveyed the foredeck's macabre tableau, Father stood and placed a hand on the helm and watched as all of their guns swerved in his direction.

Afterward, cleaned and manacled, he faced the Dutch commander: a tall, handsome, broad-shouldered man named Kurt Vanderhooven. He had full lips and a large broken nose and wore a uniform that was clean and sober. I was seated in a chair next to Father. My feet did not reach the floor.

"I find your tale hard to believe," Kurt said in English.

"Every word is true," Father replied.

"If you swear to it, I will remove the chains."

"I swear it," Father replied.

"Free his hands," said the commander in Dutch to a mate standing by.

I watched the mate's small, delicate hands open the lock that held the iron cuffs in place as the commander went on in English.

"I have some good news for you," he said, trying to repress a smile. "We are sailing to Hirado."

"Hirado," Father repeated.

"We are on our way to Japan."

Tears surged into my father's eyes. Now that his hands were free, he raised one and made as if to clear an irritant from his eyes.

"You are my guest," the commander continued. "I shall see that you and your daughter are well treated. And in exchange I hope you might speak well of me to the shogun."

"If the shogun permits me to see him, you have my word," Father said.

"Of course he shall see you, sir, a samurai from Sendai Castle with a tale like yours."

Before getting underway, Father watched the Dutch sailors throw the remains of the English crew overboard. He forbade me to look, but I found a way. The blood brought sharks. He later said the splashing sound the bodies made reminded him of when the pirates had done something similar two years earlier, when one of the bodies had been Caitríona's father. He was in pain that evening and tired of being captured, bound, and then released in exchange for something. He said he never wanted to sit in another sea captain's cabin.

He wondered what had become of Caitríona and the rest. He hoped beyond hope they had survived, that they had been somehow rescued as well. He could not bear the irony that it might be he and I who kept our lives, after facing that gruesome mob, while those he had fought to save perished. He said he thought of little else for the rest of our journey to Japan.

All of the Dutch sailors, Kurt Vanderhooven included, asked to hold and examine Father's swords. The initial days of our voyage with them were occupied with their bedazzlement at how one man had managed to kill so many others. His disinclination to discuss it only fueled their curiosity. The more suspicious among them whispered that the samurai might be an evil sorcerer best kept in the brig.

The two ships sailed in tandem and put in at Sri Lanka, Singapore, and Manila. Father rarely went ashore. The weather held. The skies remained clear, the winds mild and steady. The color of the sea alternated between deep blue and shades of emerald. Father spent most of his time with me, speaking to me in Japanese, playing with me. It was his most fervent hope that the screams of the men he had killed, so near to me, would dissipate with time and with the distractions of happier occasions. I can say that this was mostly true.

In a dull gray rain one day we sailed into the bay of Nagasaki and approached the shore of Hirado. I remember the smell of the land coming across the water, a smell that was a mix of pine and cedar. As we got closer to the pier and the houses near the harbor, pungent odors of dried fish took over, fish and seaweed boiled in thick iron cauldrons.

The Hirado settlement, reserved exclusively for the Dutch, was small and fortress-like. It had its own living quarters, a church, a large wharf, and warehouses. The Dutchman, as Father always called him, gave Father two letters, one addressed to the emperor in Kyoto, and another to the shogun in Edo. It was Kurt Vanderhooven's hope that one or perhaps both of these eminences might receive Father and, by reading the letters, deign to improve the Dutchman's relationship with Japanese traders on the mainland. Father dutifully copied them into Japanese, kept the originals, and accepted as well a sizeable leather wallet filled with *kobans* of gold. The commander momentarily considered keeping me hostage at the settlement—foreigners were forbidden to leave it—until Father returned with news. But the look Father gave him when the idea was aired quashed the thought at once.

"You have my word," Father said. "No further guarantee is needed."

"One more thing," the Dutchman said as we prepared to leave. "News has reached me that someone you mentioned in your tale is imprisoned nearby—the priest from Spain."

"Father Sotelo?" Father asked, caught by surprise.

"Yes, I believe so. He was handed over by Chinese merchants after being discovered on one of their ships docked nearby. He is in Omura, not far from here."

Father entrusted Kurt with a letter addressed to my great-aunt Soledad Medina, informing her of our safe arrival. Kurt, in turn, passed it along to the captain of a Portuguese ship. It sank with all hands aboard off the coast of Africa.

– X –

I n the village of Imari, Father changed one of the *kobans* for silver. He had his weapons cleaned and sharpened. We went to a bathhouse. He bought us new kimonos and sandals. He bought a new *kamishimo* and had the *mon*, the family crest used by Date Masamune's warriors, embroidered on it. His hair was washed and coiffed, and when he left the barber's, he strode about once again like a Sendai samurai.

We arrived in Omura in the evening and stayed at an inn. He found the prison the following morning and, as a samurai, gained admittance into the grounds with little trouble. Luis Sotelo was in a fetid cell with two other priests, a Dominican and a Jesuit, who were lying on their sides on the ground, facing away. The man Father had known as a boy, who had taught him Spanish and Latin and Greek, and who had waxed so proud in Sevilla and Madrid and in Rome with the pope, was now thin and haggard. When they embraced through the bars, Father had to avert his face from the stench. I stood next to him, staring.

"Padre," Father said.

"Bless you for coming," the priest replied. "How did you know?"

"I have only just arrived myself," Father said. "This is my daughter. I am taking her to meet my mother."

"And Guada?"

"She died giving birth."

"No."

Father said nothing.

"Has the child been baptized?" the priest asked, smiling at me.

"Yes," Father said. "I permitted it as a gesture for her great-aunt. She was baptized in the Guadalquivir like her mother."

"Bless you," said the soiled priest, looking at me.

"How can I be of help?" Father asked.

"We are fed. They allow us to pray. Our fate rests in the hands of the shogun. There is nothing you can do."

"I will ask Date Masamune to speak with the shogun on your behalf."

"I believe he has already done so," the priest said.

Father let this sink in. He told me that evening that if this were true, and the priest was still imprisoned, it did not bode well.

"You should not have returned here," Father said. "You were warned against it."

"I had no choice, my son. God wants me here."

"But not the shogun."

"The shogun's realm is fleeting," said the priest. "God's is infinite."

It had been many months since Father had listened to words like these. They reminded him of how much he rejected the Christian credo. But he respected Luis Sotelo in spite of the man's all-consuming faith.

"It pains me to see you like this," Father said. "You and yours were so helpful and courteous to us in your country."

"Do not concern yourself, Shiro-san," said the priest. "It is just punishment for my sins of pride. Do you not remember my grand scheme? How I was going to get permission and funds from the Holy Father to build my cathedral in Sendai, how I would be made the Archbishop of Japan? It was all I cared about. The quality of my new robes, the thick ring I would wear, the deference that would be shown to me in Madrid and at the Vatican, the thousands of converts I would have kneeling before my throne. Now I have returned to a life of prayer and penance."

"I remember," was all Father could think to say.

"Life is short," the priest said. "It is but a test for our eternal salvation. I thank God for having knocked me down in time to save myself. What is your little girl's name?"

"Soledad María."

"Soledad María," he repeated. "What a beautiful name."

I smiled at him.

"You know, Father, in a very real way she owes her existence to you," Father said.

"Her existence is thanks to our Lord Jesus," the priest replied.

"Might we put the Lord Jesus aside for just a moment?" Father said in a gentle tone. "It was you who taught me Spanish, you who inspired the journey to Spain. Without those things I never would have met and courted her mother."

The priest smiled and beckoned for me to approach him. His teeth were yellow. He put his thin hand with its dirty nails through the bamboo bars.

"The kingdom of heaven belongs to such as these," he said.

Father told me it was all right to give the priest my hand. When I did, he got down on his knees and kissed it.

Father never saw him again. A year later he was burned at the stake.

***

We boarded a ferry and crossed the Ariake Sea to Nagasu. We crossed the mountains to reach Kitakyushu and sailed across the Suo-nada Sea to Hiroshima. In Hiroshima, Father changed more money and took me to a puppet show. Out in the countryside he found an agreeable inn where we rested for three nights. The inn was built next to a hot spring and there were natural baths. Servant girls helped him care for me and convinced him to give me a Japanese name. He decided to call me Masako, which means "a proper child," and they organized a small party to celebrate it, and that night one of the servant girls stayed with him.

In the morning I asked him if the servant girl was to be my new mother. He laughed and told me no, that I only had one true mother, who was dead and who he would always love until he himself died. The idea of him dying upset me and I began to cry. He promised me that such an event was far, far away, and he told me to not be concerned about it. He told me that Caitríona had been a wonderful mother as well, and that one day we might hope to see her and to be with her again and with the child she bore. Then he put his hands on my shoulders and said that now we were in Japan, and that we must devote ourselves to being *there*, and to seeing what fate had in store for us.

In Fukuyama, he bought a horse and saddle. In Okayama, he bought a handsome scabbard for his katana, his long sword, a *yohon-higo* bow, and a quiver filled with arrows. As he practiced with the bow, he told me about the red leather quiver given to him by the king of Spain that he had left with Soledad Medina at La Moratalla. After reaching the town of Himeji, we went inland, and as we left the prefecture of Hyogo and approached the prefecture of Kyoto we passed through a series of roadblocks, and at each one, after he told the guards our story, they let us pass.

– XI –

Kyoto was the imperial capital where the emperor resided. To get there required a significant detour from our destination, Sendai. But Father had promised the Dutchman, and the gold Kurt Vanderhooven had given him restored the trappings of Father's status and provided us with food and lodging. He was curious to see what remained of the Heian Palace where the emperor ruled from his Chrysanthemum Throne. Fires had destroyed most of it in the twelfth century, but much of its former grandeur was said to remain. He also believed that, at my impressionable age, the more I saw of Japan and learned of its history, the better. After a Spain I hardly recalled, a year in Venice already receding, and almost two years of travel, I was ready to immerse myself in one culture, one language, one way of being.

The emperor, Go-Mizunoo, had no knowledge of the delegation Father had traveled with to Spain and Italy six years earlier. It had been conceived and funded by the now deceased shogun, Tokugawa Ieyasu, and by his son, the current shogun, Tokugawa Hidetada. Then it was organized and outfitted by Father's lord and uncle, the powerful but distant daimyo from the north, Date Masamune. The emperor had no interest in these matters. Reduced to a figurehead by the warlords, he dedicated his time to poetry, calligraphy, and ceremonial duties. Even though his wife, the empress, was the daughter of the shogun, Go-Mizunoo made a point of eschewing the shogunate's cruder approach to life. That he lived thanks to the military might of Tokugawa Hidetada was humiliating enough; to pay attention to their mundane pursuits was beneath him.

49

***

The city was humid and filled with hundreds of Buddhist temples and Shinto shrines. Half the people we saw in the streets were monks and nuns. Father took me to see the Ryoan-ji temple where an old Zen garden had been rebuilt. We sat on a wooden floor in the shade, facing thousands of pebbles raked around nine stones that represented a story about tiger cubs crossing the great waters. I asked him what the story meant. He had no idea. It was hard for me to sit still.

Father submitted the Dutchman's letter at the palace's entrance, where it was copied and returned with much bowing. He was told to wait for a response that would be forthcoming in a matter of days. But the message got no further than the second level of the emperor's administration. The response, elaborately sealed and signed by a bureaucrat who had never set eyes on Go-Mizunoo, was a screed full of vagaries. Having it in hand, Father considered his Kyoto obligations concluded, and he made preparations for us to set out for Edo, where the shogun ruled. Just before gathering me in his arms to put me in the saddle, many trumpets began to sound and people made way for an elaborate procession. It was preceded by scores of Shinto priests and Buddhist monks who were followed by the emperor's guards and bannermen. They surrounded two elaborate palanquins containing the emperor and the empress. Father asked the innkeeper what was happening.

"The Royal Family is setting out for the shrine in Nikko, in the prefecture of Tochigi," the short, squat man replied. "They are to pay homage at a new temple where the remains of the former shogun, Tokugawa Ieyasu, are buried. The current shogun will leave Edo in a few days to meet them in the town of Takasaki, along with many of the most powerful and illustrious daimyos."

Thus it was that Father decided to follow the grand procession that moved like an army and included many samurai and carts drawn by oxen loaded with food and tents and bedding.

The imperial contingent arrived at the town of Hikone two days later. There, the emperor inaugurated the completion of a castle built on the eastern shore of Lake Biwa. The fortress was both massive and delicate and was surrounded by a moat. Its construction had been initiated by a man famous for his scars and for the blood-red armor his Hikone samurai wore into battle. When word spread of Father's story and of his kinship with Date Masamune, he was taken to meet the castle builder's son. The son insisted that Father join his retinue, which was part of the emperor's procession. These samurai, still arrayed in the red armor that honored the memory of their lord, befriended Father and shared their servants and maids with us for the rest of the journey.

On our last evening in Hikone, Father took me with him to the edge of the lake. The sky had taken on a shade of deep violet. Venus shone with prominence. Father recalled the Biwa seeds his mother had given him before he left Japan and that he had given in turn to my mother. Some of them were planted at her grave at La Moratalla. He told me that now that he was back in Japan, he realized it was in Spain that he had learned to think as an independent man. And yet he had sworn to return here, had sworn to return to his mother, had sworn fealty to Date Masamune. If his word had no substance, what kind of man would that make him? He said these things to me when I was still very young, as if in apology. I did not understand his emotions. Though I still missed Caitríona, I was happy to be there, happy to receive his confidences, happy to begin learning about the land where he was born.

– XII –

The emperor's procession traveled inland along the Nakasendo Road. Our horse trotted in unison with those of the Hikone samurai. They rode upon small steeds with braided manes and tails. Some of the samurai held spears with banners attached that rippled in the mountain breeze. Steep rises of rocky land were covered in pine. In the distance the peak of Mount Ontake, covered in snow, was clearly visible. We passed a line of wooden privies being used by samurais from another domain. Jokes were exchanged. The cold air helped dissipate the odor. Father told me that farmers would come to collect the droppings for fertilizer.

He noticed that all of the red leather armor surrounding us was smooth and free from wear, and that the swords in their scabbards bore subtle but telltale signs of disuse.

"When was the last time your men saw battle?" he asked the warrior riding next to us.

"There has been no fighting since the Siege of Osaka," replied the samurai, a man some forty years of age. "Tokugawa Ieyasu won the peace on the battlefields, and now his son Hidetada preserves it. We continue to train, to put on exhibitions, some of us aid the magistrates doing police work, others have gone into business or taken up hobbies. Most of us just try to not get fat and live as best we can."

Father said that he had fought and used his sword those past six years, living outside of Japan, far more than these brothers in arms had.

"And shall the peace continue?" he asked. "Are there not rivalries and renegades causing trouble somewhere?"

52

"Very few," the older samurai replied. "You have been born into a peaceful age, young man, and have returned home at a propitious moment. You and your daughter can look forward to long and prosperous lives. You must find yourself a wife."

***

Days later we arrived in Takasaki. The town was decorated with hundreds of flags and lanterns. The inns of the bordello district were completely full. Acting and puppet troupes abounded. Festive meals were held between daimyo allies and rivals. When the shogun arrived from Edo with his large contingent, he was met with an exaggerated fanfare that pleased the empress and irritated the emperor.

One evening, the head of the Hikone samurais strode into the enclave where his men were resting and invited Father to accompany him. To my surprise, Father took me with him. We crossed through many camps and many lanes posted with armed guards before arriving at the camp of the shogun. Father stayed close to his host and did as he was told, bowing to one official, then to another. Finally, we were shown past the *Hakamoto* guards of the shogun into the private residence that Tokugawa Hidetada had commandeered. Two daimyos were exiting the reception hall as we were led in. One of them looked at me and laughed, but not in a way that was unkind.

Father bowed before Tokugawa Hidetada. I did the same. The shogun was forty-two years old then. He wore a simple black kimono and black *kamishimo*. He sat upon a square silken cushion by a hearth. Tall screens painted with seasonal blossoms were placed behind him. They concealed more bodyguards.

"Be at ease, Shiro-san," the shogun said. "Yours is my last visit of the day, so we can all have something to eat and drink. Who is this young lady you bring with you?"

"She is my daughter, my lord."

"From whence does she come?"

"From Spain, my lord, from across two oceans."

This provoked a murmur that spread through the room, and everyone leaned forward to look at me very carefully. Women appeared carrying trays with food, and wine made from rice. The women kept their gazes fixed upon the floorboards.

"I have heard a summary of your tale," the shogun said after downing a cup of the wine, "but I wish to hear it from you, from start to finish."

And so Father told his story once again, from the very beginning until his arrival in Hikone. The only details he omitted were his original vow to be the eyes and ears of Date Masamune on the journey to Europe, and his recent involvement with Caitríona. He was careful to explain his reasons for not returning to Sendai years ago with Hasekura Tsunenaga. He made it clear that Hasekura Tsunenaga had granted him permission. He was also critical of the six samurai who had chosen to remain in Spain, the ones who had settled in the little village of Coria del Río.

"Yes," said the shogun when Father finished. "We had a full report from Hasekura Tsunenaga upon his return, and he did make mention of your special relationships, especially with the Spanish, and the favor shown to you by their king. We are pleased you have returned to us, and pleased you have decided to raise your child where she belongs. We are pleased as well to have you with us here today, to visit and honor the tomb of my father, the man most responsible for your adventures."

Father was relieved and took a deep breath. He chose that moment to mention the Dutchman's letter, and an official took it from him, sticking it into his kimono before backing away. Then the shogun spoke again. "Tell me, Shiro-san, after such a long time away, do you still swear fealty to Date Masamune, you who have traveled so far while he has traveled so little?"

"Travel and time have nothing to do with such a solemn duty," Father replied. "I owe him the fealty a son owes a father. I have felt his protection and his spirit within me at all times, and I have striven to honor him with all of the foreigners that have crossed my path."

"And if I were to tell you that your lord has fallen into dishonor? Would you still revere him?" the shogun asked.

"I would defend him with my life," Father said without hesitation.

Then he bowed, looking worried.

It was then that Date Masamune stepped out from behind one of the screens. The shogun and his men all grinned and began to laugh. Father looked up. This was the first time I saw my great-uncle. His head was bare and his hair was streaked with gray. His stature emanated severity and authority. He had only one eye. Where the other had been, there was a scar. He scared me. He looked at Father and bowed to him. Father bowed back, fighting tears.

"Welcome home, Shiro-san," Date Masamune said. "My sister and I have missed you."

– XIII –

When my Japanese grandmother, Mizuki, first saw me, she recited the following poem. It was composed in the Nara Period by Okura.

Shirokane mo
Kugane mo tama mo
Nanisemu ni
Masareru takara
Koni shikame yamo

What are they to me,
Silver, or gold, or jewels?
How could they ever
Equal the greater treasure
That is a child? They cannot.

I remember how she took me to the baths that were reserved for noblewomen, holding my hand. She took me in the heavy heat of summer, in the briskness of autumn, in the snow-tinged cold of winter, and under the rains of spring. I remember the *clip-clop* sound of our wooden sandals, the caresses of the women, their smiles and comments as they examined me and watched me grow. Mizuki's body was long and beautiful, and as I got older mine followed in suit. I remember the scrubbed kimonos stretched out to dry in the sun, and the garden snake that appeared one day, causing great squealing and laughter. I remember the different bodies, the young ones and the old.

Mizuki taught me calligraphy and how to play the Satsuma Biwa lute. We wrote poetry together in the *waka* style that was beginning to fall out of fashion in those years. Father insisted I continue to learn Spanish and English. He imparted these lessons to me each day, no matter what else he did. He gained back the weight he had lost. It was good for me to see mother and son reunited. Mizuki smelled like new roses. Father smelled like hay and wood.

I remember being picked up by Date Masamune, his deep bellow of amusement whenever I ran my fingers over the scar where his eye had been. I remember the immensity of his castle where we lived, the splendor of it. I was the pet of everyone then, the exotic niece of the daimyo. My cat was gray and white and named Aiko. Some of the women called me by this name as well. I was given a hand-maiden, a young girl from a *gōnō* family in the countryside who had come to serve in our *buke yashiki,* the household of a samurai. Her name was Nobuko.

Owing to my mixed parentage, Father and Mizuki feared I might be shunned. But the affection shown to me by Date Masamune, and then the young woman I grew into, even though my hair was a shade of chestnut and my eyes gray-green, assured acceptance. And as word spread of Father's exploits in the West, our position rose higher still.

Soon after our arrival, we visited Hasekura Tsunenaga. It was shortly before his death. Apart from the priest, Luis Sotelo, he was the only other person in Japan who had known my mother. Father and he had started out as enemies on the voyage to Spain, but over time they became friends. The Hasekura house was in a wood by a lake. They gave me rice cakes, and afterward I was encouraged to feed a family of ducks at the water's edge with Nobuko, while the two men reminisced and drank sake. I heard them laughing, even though Hasekura Tsunenaga was short of breath. The Hasekura family line was old, and the women of the house severe. Some had blackened their teeth in the traditional way. None of them smiled at me.

A month later, on a cold, rainy morning, I accompanied Father, Mizuki, and Date Masamune to Hasekura Tsunenaga's funeral. Later that evening, I heard Father and my grandmother having a conversation that would, in one form or another, be repeated numerous times during the following years.

"One day," she said, "my brother will die, and I shall die."

"Even I shall die, Mother," Father said.

"My question is, what shall become of Masako?" she said. "She will be absorbed into Sendai life as a wife or a courtesan, and in old age, with luck, retire to a Buddhist nunnery."

Father had not told her of the promise he made to Soledad Medina, to bring me back to Spain.

"Soon after we returned here," Father said, "I felt regret. I felt torn and confused. I was home, had brought my daughter home. I had fulfilled my promise to you and to my uncle. I resolved to remain faithful to the warrior's way. And yet . . ."

"And yet?" she said.

"In their mind and heart and spirit, none of the other samurai I traveled with to Spain—save for those few who stayed behind—truly left these shores," he said. "Hasekura Tsunenaga was like that. What maintained his sanity while pretending to worship their crucified savior, while eating the food that never agreed with him, was his unbreakable connection with *here*. But it was different for me. I felt at home there too. It was only with the death of Masako's mother that I truly decided to return here, to recapture something,

something that was mine, and missing. I could not have lived with myself had I not seen you again, Mother, and placed Masako in your care."

"And yet?" she insisted.

"And yet like you," he said, "I wonder. I, too, think of Masako's future."

He never told her, or anyone in Japan, about Caitríona. And he would only remind me about the other child he left inside her, something I had blocked from my childhood memory, ten years later.

– XIV –

One day, Father asked Date Masamune about a young woman he had known in the daimyo's service before his journey to Spain. Her name was Yokiko. My grandmother told me Yokiko had been taken as a prize after a battle, that she was beautiful and came from a noble family, and that Date Masamune had kept her as an occasional mistress, for himself and his sons. She was the first woman Father had been with. Date Masamune told Father that Yokiko was living within the household of the daimyo's eldest son, Date Tadamune.

With the exception of the samurai in his immediate employ, Date Tadamune was not popular in Sendai. Whenever the daimyo traveled to Edo or Kyoto, Date Tadamune was left in charge. His mean character elicited embitterment from the citizens. It was a source of woe to his father, who struggled to alter his son's spiteful ways. What made things more difficult was that the daimyo's wife, Megohime, strongly supported their son. Father and Date Tadamune were educated and brought up together, but they grew apart as they grew older. Father's intelligence and physical grace, his modesty and skill with the sword, were in stark contrast to Date Tadamune's ill-shaped physique and lazy ways. That Date Masamune preferred his bastard nephew over his own son was a source of friction that was plain to all.

When Father learned of Yokiko's whereabouts he was unhappy, but he bowed to Date Masamune and said nothing. That would have been the end of it had Date Tadamune not ordered the young woman's crucifixion less than a year later. The news spread quickly.

Date Tadamune had tired of Yokiko because she repeatedly refused to please him as he wished. As punishment, he sent her to a common brothel, but she refused to participate. He then dictated her crucifixion on the grounds of adultery. She was tied to bamboo poles and hoisted up and two spears were left leaning against the poles so that anyone passing by might stab her if they wished.

When word of this reached our apartments within the castle, Father left in a fury. He arrived at the execution ground just as a samurai in Date Tadamune's service was preparing to pierce Yokiko's flesh. A group of men were gathered round, cheering the warrior on. Father called out to them and the jeering stopped. The only thing that could be heard in the sudden silence was Yokiko's moaning. Father challenged the samurai holding the spear, slicing it in half with his sword. The warrior slinked away, muttering threats of revenge, and the crowd dissipated. Father cut Yokiko down and carried her back to us. Mizuki said nothing and took her in as Father demanded and tended to her. I sat with her until she fell asleep. Father and Mizuki waited to see what would happen.

Date Tadamune complained to his father, demanding justice. The violence of the argument that ensued between them was heard throughout the castle grounds. The sniveling son put Date Masamune in a difficult position. The daimyo decided that, instead of summoning Father to be rebuked in the presence of the furious heir, he would send his closest advisor to come to our quarters and settle things. This man was Katakura Kojuro, Grandmother's former lover and, presumably, Father's real father.

They invited him in. Mizuki prepared tea. They sat in the traditional way, facing each other. It was the first time the three of them had ever been alone together. Katakura Kojuro and Mizuki had not seen each other in twenty years.

"Shiro-san," Katakura Kojuro said to my father, feigning great gravity. "You have committed a grave offense against your cousin, the heir apparent."

"What have I done?" Father asked.

"You know very well what you have done," Katakura Kojuro replied. "You have freed of your own accord a prisoner condemned to death."

"Condemned unjustly," Father said. "Only the daimyo can level such a sentence. What does my uncle say?"

"He says you must relinquish the woman and return her to Date Tadamune."

"I suggest a third way," Father said. "I propose she be sent to live out her days in Edo, in a temple as a nun, where she can atone for her acts of disobedience."

Katakura Kojuro sighed and drank his tea. Then he looked at Mizuki. She sensed his gaze and raised her head to meet it. Once they had spent years seeing each other clandestinely. They had conceived Father, who grew into a man, the man sitting there with them. But no one said anything about this.

"I will pass on your suggestion to the daimyo," Katakura Kojuro said.

During this conversation, I sat next to the sleeping Yokiko. Aiko, my cat, had settled into a circle upon the covers at the foot of the mattress. Yokiko looked tired and thin. She was still very beautiful, with a small mole on the right side over her upper lip. I held her hand. From where I sat, I could see my handmaiden in the garden pulling weeds. Within the hour, Katakura Kojuro returned, looking even more beleaguered. Once again, the three of them sat facing each other.

"Your suggestion is not acceptable," he declared.

"Can you do me the honor of explaining the decision?" Father asked.

"The daimyo was in agreement at first, but the heir apparent refused, and insists that such a choice would set a bad precedent. The daimyo came around to that opinion as well."

"Then there is another solution I shall take upon myself," Father said.

"Whatever it is, I do not recommend it, Shiro-san," Katakura Kojuro replied.

"I shall marry her," Father said.

All of us heard this; Katakura Kojuro and Mizuki who raised their heads in alarm, Yokiko who was then awake, Nobuko, and me. Even the cat was roused out of its slumber.

"Tell my uncle and my cousin I am prepared to beg at their feet for her absolution, so that I might take her as my wife," Father continued.

Father was forced to beg for Yokiko's pardon numerous times before it was granted. No one outside of our immediate family attended the wedding. Mizuki did not look at the bride. But I was pleased by the food and a new kimono that was pink with little white flowers embroidered into it. Yokiko had recovered by then and looked very beautiful, and she wept throughout the ceremony. Father wore his best robes and comported himself with great dignity.

Yokiko and Mizuki vied to be my mother. Though they often fought, both were kind to me over the years that followed, and they taught me many things. Most of the time Yokiko did her best to please Mizuki, consenting to her smallest whim. But Mizuki never accepted her, and this made Father angry, and the household was never the same.

Mizuki taught me how to dress and walk properly. She taught me how to arrange my hair. She taught me how to cut and arrange flowers and how to make rice, serve tea and sake. She taught me how to bow in a way that was modest but not subservient, the way she bowed. She taught me how and when to use a fan. She took me to Nogaku and Kyogen plays, and explained the meaning of the different masks, the gestures, and the costumes I would later try to copy. Back home in the castle I would force Nobuko to act the plays out with me in front of Mizuki and Yokiko and Father.

As I grew older, Yokiko taught me more intimate things, things that Mizuki never talked about in front of me. She taught me about men and how to tell the good ones from the bad. When my breasts began to form and when I began to bleed each month, she told me not to worry. She told me why it happened, how to clean myself properly, and what to take for the pains. She took Nobuko and me to puppet and kabuki shows.

On the occasion of my twelfth birthday, both Date Masamune and Date Tadamune came with gifts. Yokiko hid herself. One of the gifts from Date Tadamune was a *kaiken*, a small dagger traditionally given to girls upon entering womanhood. It was a very valuable one, and deadly. It is kept close to a woman's bosom to be used to either defend her honor or, failing that, to kill herself with afterward. The heir apparent lingered longer than the rest, and just before leaving he told Father that when I came of age in three years' time, he would grant us the privilege of taking me as one of his consorts. They almost came to blows. On the following day, Father made a decision.

– XV –

When Father began to learn to use a sword, the katana, he was ten years old. The man who taught him had fought in many battles waged by Date Masamune. Though there did exist a rare but real tradition of female warriors, most notably during the Heian Period, this master of the sword had never seen one. Father spent many days convincing him to take me on. A noble warrior once wrote, "The idea most central to the samurai is death. Life is such an ephemeral thing, especially for the samurai." This concept did not sit well with the way Mizuki and Yokiko and Nobuko were raised to live and think about their lives as women.

My teacher was over sixty years old on the day I met him. He lived a half an hour's ride from the castle. He was short—shorter than I—bald, and had a round belly. He brooked no concessions. He insisted I use a real sword from the very beginning. The drills he put me through, for months, were boring and relentless. He never smiled. He watched me keenly. He hit me on my hands with a rod whenever I made a mistake. Often, I would return home in tears. Mizuki and Yokiko protested to Father, but he was not perturbed and he did all he could to humor and encourage me.

My lessons began early in the morning. In the afternoons we would switch to the short sword or *tanto*, or to the spear-like weapon, the *naginata*. My teacher was graceful, and this taught me something. It taught me never to trust my first impressions of people. That such a heavy, elderly man, so severe in demeanor, could turn into a dancer, a swordsman with rapid, precise movements, and then laugh sometimes until he cried, was a revelation to me.

For hours at a time I would "slice the reed." This was a short section of green bamboo placed at eye level on a narrow platform. The idea was to cut through it at a very exact angle, again and again. If it fell to the ground it was incorrect. If the angle was off the slightest bit, it meant that, had it been a person, great and unnecessary pain would be caused. It took months before I got it right, so that I could do it with my eyes shut. I had never known such satisfaction.

After a year, he put me up against a young samurai in training. I won. When he thought me too pleased with myself, *he* went at me, and I lost. Until one day, I didn't. On that day I did not smile or express any excitement. I simply bowed to him. On that day he said to me, "You are your father's daughter." On that day I realized I was no longer learning to please my father, but to please myself.

Another man taught me the art of the bow and arrow. Still another taught me to ride like a samurai. Mizuki was vexed. She felt as if all the training she gave me in feminine comportment, music and poetry, would be for naught. She thought that no nobleman would wish to marry a girl so adept in the arts of war. But Father was content. Date Masamune was regularly informed about my progress and pretended to ignore it. Date Tadamune was kept in the dark.

While learning to wield the long sword and the short sword, the bow and the spear, I also took classes in *kyusho-jitsu* with a master who was related to the defeated Takeda clan. In addition, I became skilled at *atemi*, vital point striking and joint locking, arts designed for samurai who lost their weapons, arts that Father largely ignored.

One day, when all of my teachers agreed I was ready, Father and I went with them deep into the countryside. I could not be made a samurai officially, but they treated me that day as if it were so. Each of them gave me a bracelet to remember them by, and we celebrated by drinking sake. I heard many war stories that night. On the following day they left me alone in the woods. I was instructed to remain there for three nights, to meditate, and to hunt my own food.

My long sword, a gift from Father, was new and of the highest quality. My bow and arrows were new. My horse was young and strong. During those days and nights, alone in the woods, I meditated on all that had happened to me, to Father, to my mother, on how far I'd come. I embraced my father's heritage and made it my own. I killed a small deer, gutted and skinned it, roasted and ate it. The words the noble warrior had written, about life's ephemerality, came back to me. I had caused the beautiful animal pain. I had ended its time on this Earth. I had hunted it the way mountain cats hunt rabbits and rodents. I watched the life go out of it and was ashamed. I bowed to it and swore I would only do so again if my own life depended on it. I bowed to the trees, to the moss, to the earth, to the boulders, and to the stream.

I returned to the castle a different person.

— XVI —

As my training continued during my thirteenth and fourteenth years, poems and gifts from Date Tadamune arrived regularly. Everyone agreed that the quality of the poems was too fine to have originated from his pen. Mizuki and Father were alarmed. Yokiko, feeling responsible, withdrew into herself. It was common knowledge that Tadamune was cruel to his women, and everyone in Sendai knew the resentment he felt toward Father, the vow of vengeance he'd taken in the form of a promise to have me in his bed.

Father decided to speak with the daimyo about it, and he was received in Date Masamune's private garden. When the daimyo stepped out onto the polished floorboards of the deck, just before a panel slid shut behind him, Father caught sight of a woman he recognized. It was Date Masamune's favored mistress, the woman who had first presented Father to Yokiko many years earlier. It was rumored that the daimyo had suffered a mild stroke. Mizuki denied it and said her older brother remained in perfect health. But Father looked for symptoms anyway. He did think his lord looked older. He was slightly stooped, and he was slower to sit. The malady was confirmed when his uncle began to speak. Though easy to understand, there was no doubting a slight slurring of his words.

"It has been my hope," Father said, "that your son would forget his threat, and that he would move on, to court a more suitable young woman."

"He claims to be truly taken by her," Date Masamune said. "And who would not be? Her beauty is unique, and her grace is identical to your mother's."

"We fear him, my lord," Father said. "I mean no disrespect, but were he of a more moderate character, we would be honored by such an expression of feeling."

"I know," Date Masamune said, bowing his head. "His mother, who goads him on, grows stronger as I weaken. He grows more assertive as I get older. I am at a loss."

Father was shocked by such an admission from so powerful a man. He attributed some of it to the daimyo's illness, but some of it derived as well from the level of trust and respect Date Masamune was willing to show his treasured nephew.

"I see," Father said.

"What will you do?" his uncle asked.

"I am not sure," Father replied. "I have no plan as yet. The only thing I am sure of is that I shall not, under any circumstance, permit it to happen."

"I understand," the daimyo said. "I'm told the girl is turning into a fearsome fighter, but I am not convinced of how that might be of help to her."

They both sat in silence for a moment.

"Do you recall," Date Masamune asked, "the last time we sat here together?"

"I do, my lord."

"You were the age your daughter is now. You had just become a samurai. It was the day you swore me fealty."

"The day you gave me your sword."

The daimyo smiled and looked out at the garden.

"Yes. It was the day I gave you my sword. And the day I swore I would look out for you and your descendants for as long as I lived."

"We sat facing the garden, side by side. You never looked at me. I was very nervous. You were like a god."

"That was the idea," Date Masamune said, and both of them laughed. Then he turned serious again.

"It was I who sent you to Yokiko in the first place. It was I who sent you to the foreigners on a perilous journey to the east. It was because of me you risked your life and the life of your daughter to return here."

"It is not your responsibility, Uncle. The decisions were mine."

They sat in silence again.

"Do you know what impresses, perhaps more than anything, my lord?" Father finally said. "The boulder there in the garden, and the Akamatsu tree beside it. They were here the day I became a samurai, and they are here now. During all the time, and all of the events that have transpired, since we first sat here together, the boulder and the tree have persisted, quietly, without moving."

"Or caring," Date Masamune said.

"Or caring," Father agreed.

***

Father learned later that it was after this meeting with Date Masamune that Mizuki arranged to speak with the daimyo's wife, Megohime. She suggested that since the original grievance had stemmed from the frustrated execution of Yokiko, the grievance and its associated vow of vengeance might be alleviated by revisiting the sentence of death. It was thought that Megohime discussed the idea with Date Tadamune, and that an agreement was reached. And thus it happened that I woke one morning and found Yokiko cold and still, curled into a ball, dead from poison.

I was spared the death of my mother in Spain because I was only minutes old when it happened. The loss of Maria Elena in Venice and then of Caitríona were hard, their effects difficult to gauge.

Apart from Mizuki, Yokiko was the mother I had the longest, during the years most crucial in a woman's life. Together with Mizuki, she led and guided me, from girlhood to early womanhood. That she could be alive one day, alive to the world's light and sensations, alive to her thoughts and inner yearnings, and then be dead the next, reduced to a mound of insensate hair and flesh, pained me deeply. How could life be so wondrous and yet so cruel? How could Mizuki have done such a thing?

Father was incapable of accusing his mother of such an act, but after the funeral services, after sending Yokiko's spirit to the pure land, he moved to other quarters and took Nobuko and me with him. Then, as if to double the devilry, Date Tadamune reneged on the agreement, an agreement he denied ever sanctioning. He renewed his courtship of me. As the following months passed, the poems and the gifts came more frequently. In early winter, tension reached a breaking point. Mizuki kissed me goodbye and took herself to a nunnery. In the space of a season, I had lost both of my Japanese mothers.

Before she left, Mizuki came to say farewell to her son, and told him something that shocked him. She told him that Katakura Kojuro was not, in fact, his biological father. She told him she had always been surprised by how easily people believed her cover story. "Look at you," she said to my father, "tall and slim and graceful, and then look at Katakura Kojuro, short and squat. Look at all of his other children, short and squat. I have always been flattered," she said, "to hear how everyone, including my brother, attributed your physical demeanor entirely to me. But it is not so."

Father looked at her, amazed, and said nothing.

"I did have a relationship with Katakura Kojuro. He was kind to me at a difficult time. And he does believe you are his son. But the man I loved, however briefly and even more than my first husband, was a Chinese monk—your father, who was passing through Sendai. Ingen was his name. He arrived. We loved each other. And then he departed, leaving you inside of me. He was as beautiful to look at as he was in spirit."

"Where did he go?"

"I do not know," she said. "Years later I heard he founded a temple here in the kingdom. But I do not know where, or if it is true."

"I am half Chinese," he said.

"Yes," she replied.

"Why have you never told me?"

"Because the last time we said goodbye I held on to the hope you would return," she said, her eyes welling with tears. "But this time I know we shall never see each other ever again."

She lowered her head and cried bitterly. He wanted to comfort her. She was his mother. But the murder of Yokiko hung over them both.

***

One night, after packing some clothing and gathering my weapons, after giving my cat to Nobuko, Father and I left Sendai.

– XVII –

I never remembered seeing Father use his sword. What happened
aboard that ship in the Indian Ocean was buried deep. The little
I remember from it are just sounds, because my eyes were closed.
During the many winters we lived in Sendai, he carried his treasured
katana with him often, and sometimes he would let me use it for
practice. All I knew about his fighting skills came from stories told
to me by older samurai when they drank too much. But when some
of Date Tadamune's warriors caught up with us between Misawa
and Lake Ogawara, I witnessed it firsthand.

There were ten of them. At first, they behaved with exaggerated
politeness. Their code demanded it, and they had been sworn to
bring me back unscathed. But Father refused their entreaties, bowed,
and unsheathed his sword. I, too, unsheathed mine. This caused
Date Tadamune's men to laugh, and Father took advantage of their
mirth by attacking first. I had never seen such classic, sober swords-
manship put to such deadly effect. He killed them all, except for one
who, his right hand severed, begged for mercy. Father looked at me
and spoke calmly. "If we spare his life he will return and tell them
where we are." I approached the man and "sliced the reed." His head
rolled off of him. I shall never forget the noise it made hitting the
hardened wintry earth.

After that, as we continued north toward Mutsu on the bay,
heading for Oma, we spoke very little. He had first thought to ask
the shogun to intervene on my behalf, but decided against it, thinking it might be interpreted as a gesture of disrespect toward Date
Masamune. Father was thirty-seven years old that year. He was not

the eighteen-year-old samurai who had landed in Spain and courted my mother. Killing Date Tadamune's men after so many years of peaceful life in Sendai, casting himself out as a renegade, a ronin on the road, traveling light with a fifteen-year-old girl into an uncertain future, must have weighed upon him. Seeing him kill all those men, and my own beheading of a samurai who had begged for mercy, weighed upon me as well. And he knew it. But we did not speak of it.

Another thing I never spoke about to him was how flattered I had been by the poems and gifts sent to me by Date Tadamune. I confess that back then, the idea of living in his household, of sharing his bed upon occasion, filled me with excitement. One day he would become the daimyo of Sendai, which up until then had been my world. As for his bad reputation with respect to women, I, in my youth, and with what Yokiko had taught me, was certain I could reform him. I even found his lack of physical appeal easy to ignore, for his robes were sumptuous and his manner that of a man accustomed to great luxury.

In Oma we boarded a small ship north, to the island of Ezo, where the Ezochi people lived. They were a race of fishermen who worshipped nature, and who kept themselves separate from the Japanese, toward whom they harbored centuries of suspicion. We did not stop traveling until we found a small village on the sea near the town of Nemuro, just as the snows began.

It was clear to the villagers that Father was a runaway samurai and a man of stature. Once they learned I was his daughter and not his wife, and as he began to speak with them more, and help them with their fishing in exchange for food and a roof over our heads, bonds were formed. It was not until the third large snowstorm that blanketed the thatch-roofed houses and narrow streets that I mustered the courage to ask him what we were going to do.

We were sitting by the hearth in the middle of the room, where an iron pot simmered with fish and herbs. Outside the wind howled.

"I thought we might stay here for the rest of our lives," he said. "And you could marry one of the fishermen, and have many babies, and spend your days mending nets and cooking seaweed."

I looked at him in the flickering light, holding my breath, until he began to laugh.

"Perhaps not," he said, stirring the pot with his short sword. "After all, I am a prince and you a noblewoman with an inheritance to claim, in a part of the world where women are not crucified for refusing to work in a brothel."

"Spain," I said.

"Spain," he replied.

"But it is so very far away," I said. "How could we possibly get there? It is against the law for us to leave these islands."

"The distance is the problem," he said, "not the law. We are already outlaws here."

He used the word *muhōmono*, meaning fugitive or bandit, and I liked the way it sounded.

"It is a long and perilous journey which I have taken twice in my life," he said. "Despite my promise to your great-aunt, it is one I had hoped never to take again. But it was a mistake to bring you here. I apologize to you from the bottom of my heart, Masako. Now it is time to fulfill that other promise I made, some thirteen years ago, even though it was to someone surely buried by now."

He spoke these words with such solemnity that I began to cry. The snow, the wind, the meagerness of the dwelling, the isolation of the village, the primitive people who lived there, the two women I loved who had taken such good care of me and who were so far away that night, one of them cremated—it all crushed down upon my heart. Father let me cry. The only other thing he said that night was,

75

"I shall find a way." Just before I fell asleep, I told him how much I missed Yokiko and Mizuki and Nobuko and my cat and all of the things we had left behind in Sendai. He rubbed my back until the wind died, until all that could be heard were the waves of the sea breaking in the darkness under the falling snow, until at last I fell asleep.

– XVIII –

In the spring an Ezochi elder came to the village and told us that more samurai had landed to the south, near Tomakomai, and that they were looking for us. Father was grateful and told the man we would leave the following day so as not to bring trouble upon them. This led to a long discussion with the elder about who we were, and how we had come to be there, and where it was we wished to go.

"I need to return to the Dutch enclave on the island of Hirado, in the hope of finding a ship sailing for Europe."

"Where is Europe?" the elder asked.

"It is a land far in the east, filled with barbarians of great wealth," Father replied. "But as I am a wanted man, we cannot reach Hirado traversing the islands of Japan. I could try and get there by sea, but they shall be looking for us along the coast as well. I could go west, but I speak little Chinese and it would take a lifetime to cross all of China and the lands beyond it before reaching Europe."

"I know nothing of Europe," the elder said. "But I do know how to reach the lands east of us."

The elder then spent a night consulting with the men in his party. Their decision to help us was not entirely based on goodwill. Some merchants from Japan were making inroads in their markets and some of the Ezochi leaders were garnering wealth. Though they were decent enough to not turn us in, they were eager to be rid of us. On the following morning the elder showed us a map Father had never seen before. It showed Japan and, just to the east, across a stretch of sea not unduly vast, another large landmass.

"Fifteen years ago, we thought one of our best sailors had perished with his fishing boat in a great storm," the elder said. "But six months later he returned and told us of another land the winds had pushed him to, a land with vast harbors and friendly natives, and coasts filled with whales and seals. A month later we sent three of our largest fishing boats with him, and found it to be true. Since then we have started a small colony there. After communicating with the natives, we drew this map to show them how their land occupies the Earth."

Father studied the map and realized the landmass in question belonged to a place his ship had stopped on the original voyage to Europe, a place they had rested after crossing a much wider part of the ocean. He saw this was a shorter route, and on the map at least, it looked as if the distance one would need to travel to cross this new landmass, and reach the island of Cuba, was something he and I might be able to do. The elder spoke to Father again.

"If you swear not to tell another living soul about our colony there, we can put you on our next ship sailing there."

"I swear it," Father said, putting his hand to his heart.

"Then gather your things," the elder said, "for the ship sails in three days, and it will take us two to reach the harbor."

– PART THREE –

PART THREE

In Spain, my mother had an older brother, Carlos Bernal Fernández de Córdoba y de la Cerda. But I shall simply call him Carlos. Under normal circumstances, he would have been the sole inheritor of his family's great wealth and properties. But shortly before my mother's unfortunate marriage, Carlos entered a monastery. Second-born and third-born young men of noble Spanish families, disadvantaged by the laws of primogeniture, often entered the priesthood. After taking the sacrament of Holy Orders, they served as influential confessors at court. Some kept mistresses and had children. The upper strata of society accepted it. But it was unusual for a firstborn son like Carlos to study for the priesthood. In households as distinguished as his, it would be regarded as a great sacrifice, a refusal of the riches of this world in exchange for an eternal life of grace in the next.

According to Caitríona, my uncle Carlos claimed he *did* have a true calling, for a time. Though his days in the seminary were constrained by a routine of relative austerity, his spiritual life blossomed. He found himself surrounded by others of his age and station endowed with similar passions. But after three years, as his preparation to take the sacrament reached its culmination, he experienced a change of heart. He told Caitríona that alone in his cell one night, gazing at the moon, he realized he could not see it through, and he resolved to return to society.

By the time he left the seminary, my mother was dead and his parents had already willed the bulk of their estates and possessions to my mother's first child, Rodriguito, who had been left in their care. Carlos and his father, Don Rodrigo, had never gotten along, and Don Rodrigo viewed his son's decision to leave the seminary with suspicion and irritation. His mother, Doña Inmaculada, was more sympathetic, but there was little she could do to change her husband's mind. In truth, neither of them was especially concerned with Carlos' religious dilemmas. They were more perturbed by his tastes for questionable romantic entanglements. Upon his liberation, Doña Inmaculada encouraged him to find a proper Sevillana and marry as soon as possible.

He was gently but firmly banished to Carmona, where he was assigned the task of managing the family's estate there. "Your mother," my grandfather said to him, "makes an appearance there twice a year, entranced within a mist of memories from her childhood, and she does little that is useful, other than check the linen and hand out alms to beggars. I am quite certain we are being robbed in a most disrespectful and wanton manner, each and every year, by our farmers, laborers, and household help, all of whom have little incentive to do otherwise. Look into it, son. Keep your eye on them. Exert a presence. Insist upon accounts rendered, and double-check them. Order any necessary repairs or improvements, and make sure they are done, and done at the amounts agreed upon. Let them know we are a family that is not to be trifled with. And if you must beat someone or dismiss anyone, do not hesitate. The local constables still fear and respect our coat of arms. And by all means, concentrate your energies on the females of the species."

Uncle Carlos did his best. But the initial enthusiasm he experienced at being free of the seminary, and free from his father's hectoring, soon gave way to boredom. The local gentry in Carmona were hopelessly conventional. Carlos' dandyish sense of fashion was either ridiculed or ignored. There were no local damsels that appealed to him in the least, and from time to time he imported a young friend from Sevilla, so as to not rouse the rage and scorn of his neighbors.

He played games of Ruff and Honors with the local doctor, the priest, and the chief constable, after he taught them the rules. The son of his least honest farmer was a beautiful lad he would have killed to conquer, but if word got out, Don Rodrigo would summon him back to Sevilla and never leave him in peace again.

It was at this juncture that a letter, written in my grandmother Inmaculada's elegant script, told him of his aunt Soledad Medina's declining health, along with gossip to the effect that she had taken on a new ward, a widowed foreign girl she was said to dote upon almost as much as she had upon my mother. Intrigued and in want of a change of air, he spent a week increasing demands and threats upon his workers. He gave detailed instructions to the household help as to where and how to clean, where and how to prune, where and how to primp and polish. He then gathered together his latest Parisian coats and breeches and commandeered a two-horse carriage.

Doña Inmaculada and her bevy of envious señoras from Sevilla society had been disseminating the opinion that Doña Soledad was close to madness. But Carlos had his doubts. Though a long time had passed since he had last seen her, his memories were favorable. Even a much diminished, and possibly senile, Soledad Medina would be far preferable to the company the rest of his family kept. He remembered her as being truly stylish, as opposed to Sevilla-stylish. She was multilingual, a former beauty who actually read. She had had the exquisite taste, once upon a time, to have chosen the Duke of Medina-Sidonia as her lover. Her late husband, almost as wealthy as she, had been an infamous philanderer. Reliable rumors proclaimed her last lover, many years past, was a priest she had poisoned upon discovering he was also ravishing her cook's young daughter. She had been kind to Carlos when he was a boy, and he remembered La Moratalla as a kind of Arcadia. Her two sons, his cousins now deceased, he recalled as bullies, something she had been aware of, and that she had endeavored to curtail.

Setting off at dawn, he drove the carriage north to the Guadalquivir River and followed it east through the villages of El Acebuchal, El Calonge, and Peñaflor. After leaving Palma del Río, he followed the river Bembézar as it wound its way northwest, until the sight of a pair of guards, posted at the start of a long and private tree-lined road, confirmed he had arrived. He reached the imposing gates of the estate proper just before twilight. He told me that his first impressions, seeing the gardens and the fountains, the sculptures and the main house in such magnificent condition, made him question why he had stayed away so long. It also drove home, in an instant, the distance between his immediate family's wealth, which was considerable, and that of his aunt.

A footman greeted him and installed him in a charming room decorated with various sets of antlers mounted on plaques and still-life paintings of dead game. A note from Doña Soledad requested his presence in the main drawing room for a pre-supper aperitif at nine o'clock. Though eager to wear a pair of pink satin breeches embroidered with gold stars, for finally, here was a place, though hidden deep in an unpopulated corner of rural Andalucia, where such a garment might be appreciated, he chose instead a pair more sober in hue, with a navy vest and coat.

***

At nine o'clock sharp, Doña Soledad emerged dressed in black. He noted how the dress was of the best couture. Her health had actually improved over the months Caitríona had been living with her. She no longer required the moveable chair, and relied instead on a black cane with a silver handle shaped like a wild boar. Caitríona O'Shea came into the room just behind her. He thought her beautiful, and admired her thick braided auburn hair, her brown taffeta dress and lace collar. Caitríona's Spanish had improved enough to allow conversation in the family's native tongue. Her first impression of my uncle was vivid, that he was slim and not very tall, but graced with a beautiful face, high cheekbones, brown eyes, and blond hair. The ladies drank ice-cold Manzanilla sherry, Carlos a fortified wine.

"Carlitos," Doña Soledad asked him, "how long has it been?"

"Nine years," he said. "When I was sixteen."

"*Qué barbaridad*," she replied. "Now I must congratulate you for deciding against the priesthood."

"I'm not cut out for it," he said with a smile.

"I could have told you that," she said. "You might have saved yourself the trouble if you had thought to consult me first."

"My father rather insisted upon it."

"Perhaps he hoped to have a confessor in the family," she said in jest.

"I cannot imagine an experience more onerous than having to listen to my father's sins," he replied, pleased with his wit.

She did not entirely trust his motives for the sudden visit, after so many years, but she told me she saw so much of my mother in his physiognomy, that it pleased her to look at him.

"What brings you here just now, after all this time?" she asked him.

"Where to begin?" he replied. "Ennui with my current condition, I suppose, and a sudden nostalgia for this beautiful estate, and its mistress. I would have come to you sooner, after my liberation from the cloth, but I was unable to leave Carmona until now—and when I see the wonderful state things are in here, I am tempted to kidnap your foreman, whose skills would make my newly found raison d'être much easier."

"So you've taken the reins of your mother's estate," she said, unconvinced by his elaborate flattery.

"At my father's insistence."

"Do you always do as your father bids?" Caitríona asked suddenly. "First the priesthood, now the farm?"

My uncle told me that when she said it, her impertinence surprised, annoyed, and charmed him.

"I live, quite literally, at his discretion," he said, looking at her directly for the first time. "My income comes from his pocket. It falls upon me like manna upon the desert. I imagine something similar must happen to you, here, as well."

"*Touché*," she said with a blush.

"There is nothing more vulgar than conversation about money," Doña Soledad said. "Tell us something amusing."

"Amusing," he said, searching desperately. "Well, perhaps it is not terribly amusing, but as I was savoring the aroma of the orange blossoms out my window here earlier this evening, I could not help but remember how dreadful the priests smelled when I lived with them in the monastery."

"My word," Doña Soledad replied, raising a fan to cover her nose. She feigned to be affronted so as to hide a small sore recently erupted there that she repeatedly covered with powder. But Caitríona laughed, and this pleased him.

Prompted at supper, she described some of her happier memories from her girlhood in Ireland, and Carlos appeared captivated by it. He in turn recalled how, as children, he and my mother played at hide-and-seek there at the Moratalla estate. He did not mention the misery Doña Soledad's sons caused him, but later my great-aunt told me that she remembered it while he spoke at the table that night. She remembered how sensitive he'd been as a child, and saw flickers of that same sensitivity still there, hidden by then under layers of cynicism and faux worldliness. She felt sorry for him. Everyone knew what the central drama of his life was, an issue that, in her old age, seemed trifling. She recalled the hours of handwringing and complaint she'd been forced to hear from Doña Inmaculada, and the fulminations against the Lord flung forth by Don Rodrigo for having been cursed with such a son.

It was with this proclivity of her nephew's in mind that she placed no obstacles in his path when he asked permission to accompany Caitríona the following day to visit my mother's grave. Doña Soledad was no longer able to get there, and she had Caitríona go for her each day instead. Caitríona brought bouquets of flowers, and detailed instructions for keeping the site free of weeds and fallen leaves. It was a daily excursion she enjoyed and had grown accustomed to, kneeling before the remains of my father's former love.

One night she described to me how it felt for her when the head gardener had taken her to the grave for the first time one pristine autumn afternoon. Though she had been told about the Roman columns, she was shocked to see them, and realized they had not been imported. She told me she had seen enough in her short life by then to know that what rested beneath the earth she knelt upon, that what remained of my beautiful, worshipped mother, right there so close to her knees, was something too horrible to describe—bone, sinew, darkened robes. That such macabre elements had once been a beautiful creature, filled with life and emotion, sobered her. The macerated flesh beneath the grass had known the pleasure of Father's embrace. It had captured his heart in a way she feared she hadn't. It had carried and, just before expiring, given birth to me, the child Caitríona had cared for so lovingly in Venice, in Greece, and in Egypt. The thought that she and her son were all that survived, because of the love story that had started with the corpse buried beneath her there, was doubly strange.

On the way up to the grave with Carlos, conversation was scant at first. It was not until they crossed the small wooden bridge separating the formal gardens from the wilder parts of the property that he inquired about her son.

"How do you know I have one?" she asked.

"I don't," he conceded. "It's just a rumor that reached me, in a letter from my mother. Is it true?"

"Yes," she said.

"And is he in good health?"

"In what regard?"

"I thought I would have seen him by now."

"Is that part of the rumor as well?" she asked. "That he is afflicted with some deformity?"

"Not at all," he said with a grin. "No one in Sevilla possesses that degree of imagination."

"I'm relieved to say he is in splendid health," she said, "and perhaps, before you leave, I shall present him to you."

"I'd like that," he said.

"Did you ever meet your sister's child?" she asked.

"No," he said. "I'm afraid I never did."

"Why is that?"

"I was chained to the seminary," he replied, uneasy.

"All that time?" she insisted. "The girl was almost two when her father left with her. Would you not have been allowed a dispensation?"

"I suppose I might have," he said. "But we grew apart, you see— my sister and I. All of it entirely my fault," he hastened to add. "I'm not proud of it."

"I beg your pardon," she said, blushing and looking away. "You must think me monstrous."

"Not at all."

But he probably did.

She observed his behavior at the grave. Doña Soledad, she knew, would demand a full accounting. For her own part, she decided that if my uncle shed tears, they would probably be false, and he would forfeit her interest and respect. But he didn't. He knelt down, and with his head bowed, seemed to pray. But then he became distracted by how she was arranging fresh blossoms about the headstone.

"It's good of you to have brought flowers," he said.

"I do it every day," she said, "for your aunt."

He simply nodded.

On the way back down to the formal gardens and the house, she felt a need to say more. "I know I should try to ignore it," she said, "but I am uncomfortable with the fact that people like your mother gossip about me. People who have never laid eyes on me."

"Give it no more thought," he said. "It's what people in the provinces do, everywhere really, but most especially in Sevilla."

"Even so," she said, "I would feel better if I told someone other than your aunt, you for example, my full story. I expect it will come out eventually anyway, but in some distorted fashion."

"I would be honored," he said, "and I will be very discreet."

"As if you were my confessor," she said.

He laughed. "Precisely."

And so she told him everything, with greater detail than she had ever used in her discussions with Doña Soledad, if only because he was so much closer to her in age. And when they arrived at the house, she took him to the nursery to see little Patrick. Fascinated by the child's foreign aspect, Carlos did his best to be agreeable to the little boy.

Years later my uncle confessed that when he retired to his rooms after the meal that day, he lay down and considered the possibility that his mother and her friends were correct, that his aunt might be going mad. How else to explain her attachment to the young Irish woman and her bastard child? Clearly it was yet another expression of the old woman's devotion to the memory of his dead sister. Convinced that my father and I had departed this Earth, the Irish damsel and her son were the only creatures that maintained a living link to his aunt's lost loved ones. And what a curious link it was, he thought. But then he had to admit that Caitríona seemed a pleasant young woman. She was spirited and refreshingly frank. She was a pleasure to look at, and her little boy was handsome. And so, by the time evening arrived, he thought it might behoove him to strive for some degree of the open-mindedness, some degree of the generosity, or "madness," that defined Doña Soledad. For it seemed to him that his aunt still felt sympathy toward him, and she was old and very wealthy, and—something that rarely left his mind for long—his parents were still determined to leave almost all of what should have been his to Rodriguito, my mother's little boy.

It was at that moment, he said, as the light changed, and cool air entered through the windows, when he first gave serious thought and consideration to my mother, his sister, his former playmate, to whom all the family's love and attention had transferred once his inadequacies as the firstborn became obvious. What a short and strange life she'd had. Raped by her husband. Then impregnated again by a fellow who might as well have descended from the moon, only to die giving birth to the violent foreigner's baby girl.

And he remembered how, before supper that evening, he changed into his pink breeches, if only to see how the ladies would respond. Adjacent to the full-length looking glass, where he spent a good deal of time admiring himself, he noticed something quite beautiful hanging on a peg in the corner. He went over and saw it was a leather quiver, filled with royal arrows, a very handsome quiver that had been dyed a deep, rich red. Upon returning to Carmona he took it with him.

– XX –

They were three conversations Caitríona would never forget. The first took place in the courtyard at the Casa de Pilatos, the same place where, two years earlier, she had waited with Paolo Sarpi on her first day in Sevilla. It was winter and misty. The air smelled of rose petals and burning leaves.

"You will of course be within your right to take a lover," my uncle said. "I only implore that you exercise precaution. If your honor were to be besmirched mine would be as well."

"You are most kind," Caitríona replied.

"I am serious."

"Yes. I know."

"And . . . well . . ."

"Yes?"

"Nothing," he said, flustered. "I don't know what I was going to say."

"I assure you," she said, "that nothing you declare at this juncture can shock me in the least."

"It is only that, perhaps, if you were so inclined, so disposed, if you were sufficiently taken with my person, at some moment in time," he said, "we might attempt to conceive a child together."

"I thought that was it."

"And?"

"We might. At some point. Were we both so inclined," she said. "Do not be overly concerned for me. I know what this is. It suits me. I appreciate it, if only for the welfare of my son. And I shall do all I can, within reason, to give you the propriety and the freedom you desire."

He took her hand and kissed it.

Their engagement was announced the following week. Doña Inmaculada was pleased. Don Rodrigo was suspicious, and sought his son out to have it out with him. Carlos told her what was said. It took place at Don Rodrigo and Doña Inmaculada's palace in Sevilla.

"Your mother insists I congratulate you and so I shall," Don Rodrigo had said. "But you should be aware that this most unexpected announcement will not change the intention of my will in any way. Since you seem to have the blessing of Soledad Medina, I leave it to her to bestow any additional riches upon you."

"No one is more aware of your iron will than I, sire," Carlos replied. "Once a course is chosen by you, God himself could not bend it."

"Do not blaspheme, boy."

"The blasphemy was yours, Father, in sending me to the seminary—a blasphemy that brought about my sister's marriage to a selfish brute you shared your mistress with, that led to her violation, and to her subsequent relations with the samurai, that led directly to her death. You are a fine one to accuse me of blasphemy."

Carlos was too strong and grown to receive a father's blow. Rodrigo simply turned and left the room. He did not attend the wedding, and made a point of never setting eyes on his son again. Inmaculada gave Carlos the estate in Carmona. Doña Soledad gave them a townhouse in Sevilla next to the Casa de Pilatos, thirty rooms and twelve servants, and an account set up for its permanent upkeep. Caitríona promised to remain as Soledad's companion, and did so.

Some months after the wedding, when Caitríona was alone with Doña Soledad at La Moratalla, my great-aunt engaged her in conversation as they sat outside by the main fountain, near a grove of pomegranate trees. Carlos had left them after a weeklong visit.

"Might I ask you a most personal question, Caitríona?" said my great-aunt.

"You certainly may," she replied.

"I, and a wide swath of Sevilla society, have long been privy to the particulars of Carlos'—inclinations—and I am wondering if he possessed sufficient backbone to share them with you before the wedding."

"He did, my lady."

"I see."

"Though I am still young," Caitríona said, "I have seen enough of the world to learn how to distinguish between men who prefer ladies and those who prefer the company of other men."

"Quite," Doña Soledad said before taking a sip of her favorite sherry. "In my day," she went on, "with rare and colorful exceptions, it was not so easy to make those kinds of distinctions. People one would have sworn were conventional were well skilled at procuring the sorts of companions they truly preferred. I've known many men, and women, from the most respected families, including my own, who had numerous children, but who in fact coveted most ardently members of their own sex."

"I suppose," Caitríona said, "it is possible as well to maintain an interest in both sexes. In any event, we had a very frank discussion before announcing our betrothal. I am not in love with him, nor is he with me. But we understand each other, and we have come to like each other, and we agree that the marriage is to our mutual benefit. It provides him with respectability, and it guarantees my son a certain security."

"Carlos has just been here for a week," said my great-aunt, taking another sip of her wine. "What goes on with you two at night?"

Caitríona laughed at the dowager's boldness.

"We read to each other, and talk about our lives, like good friends."

"You know," said Doña Soledad with a grin, "I can't recall the last time I had this kind of discussion, if at all. And yet it is a topic that people devote much thought to, throughout their lives."

"I have never spoken of it with anyone either," Caitríona replied. "My own mother was unapproachable with respect to these sorts of questions. The closest I ever came were a few brief discussions with the woman in Venice that Soledad María was given to, who was not a bad woman at all, but a wise and even generous lady, who had done the best she could under terrible conditions."

Doña Soledad had no desire to hear any more about the woman from Venice.

"Getting back to you, dear," she said. "I feel I must raise two issues. First—and I regret not having had this conversation before your wedding—you did not have to marry my nephew in order to secure a future for your son. You have me for that. I know I shall not be about for much longer, but I assure you I have already broached the topic of his and your welfare with my Fugger bankers."

"I am so very grateful, my lady. After all you have done for me, I simply could not find it within myself to bring such a thing up."

My great-aunt made her customary gesture, waving Caitríona's comment away.

"The second issue," she said, "is more thorny. I haven't brought it up before because of the vast amount of pain surrounding it, but as an old woman with little faith, in anything really, I have nevertheless permitted myself to consider one small detail with which I've managed to sustain my life thus far. Unless you and Signor Sarpi hid some observation even more chilling than the ones I insisted upon hearing, I've clung to what I hope is the fact that neither he nor you actually saw the deaths of the samurai and the child. Is that so?"

All the merriment within Caitríona's heart vanished as she listened to these words, and by the end she found herself weeping.

"Yes. That is true. But—"

"And I also recall," Doña Soledad continued, interrupting her, "that Signor Sarpi mentioned there were no muskets involved."

"That is true as well."

"You see what I am getting at."

"I cannot speak for you, madam," Caitríona said. "But had you been there, and seen what I was forced to see, I most seriously doubt you could harbor such a hope."

"Nevertheless, you did not see them killed," Doña Soledad said, her voice shaking.

"No, my lady."

"And so they might still return."

"Yes, my lady."

"And what would happen if they did, now that you have married Guada's brother?"

"I would curse myself, and die from happiness."

Doña Soledad took Caitríona's hand with both of hers and forcefully kissed it.

– XXI –

Then a terrible thing happened that, in many ways, should have liberated my uncle Carlos. Instead, it poisoned his soul. While Carlos was entertaining his mother at the estate in Carmona, and while Caitríona was with Doña Soledad in Sevilla, Don Rodrigo took my mother's little boy, Rodriguito, on a hunting trip. The boy was mauled by a boar, and died hours afterward, and late that same evening, insane with grief, guilt, and alcohol, my grandfather, Don Rodrigo Fernández de Córdoba, shot himself in the head. By the time Doña Inmaculada returned from Carmona, her husband and grandchild were already buried. Owing to the sinful manner of his death, it required a large donation by Doña Soledad to assure that Don Rodrigo was buried in holy ground.

The death of his father and nephew affected Carlos badly. The inheritance that had been taken from him, now restored, was not experienced as a victory. Rather than celebrate, if only inwardly, and enjoy the tragic but fortuitous twist of fate that gave him what he had always believed to be his, it increased his greed and insecurity. He began to spend more and more time in his parents' palatial house that he would now inherit along with everything else. It was only for appearance's sake that he continued to spend a few nights a week with Caitríona in the home given to them by Soledad Medina. Upon inheriting his father's position as a grandee of Spain, he was called to Madrid for an audience with the young king, Philip the Fourth. During his absence, Caitríona returned once again to the Casa de Pilatos.

Rosario Sánchez de Úbeda and her son Francisco were in Sevilla when the memorial service for Don Rodrigo and the little boy was held at the cathedral. As a young woman, Rosario had married the Duke of Medina-Sidonia, then a man forty years older than she. By the time their son Francisco was born, the duke was dead. Many women in Sevilla looked down on her—out of envy for her youth and beauty, because she was a commoner from a small village, and because she had no title. To the annoyance of Doña Inmaculada, Rosario was invited to Soledad Medina's house after the service, and it was there she met Caitríona. Though four years older than Caitríona, Rosario got on well with her. She was distraught to learn what had happened to Father and me, and even though Caitríona suspected that Rosario's grief implied an unspoken degree of intimacy with Father, she comforted her.

It was a difficult time for my grandmother. Doña Inmaculada was alone in a home she no longer owned. For the first time in her life, religion failed her. She had relied upon it in her youth, when she first realized her husband was unfaithful to her. She had relied upon it when her parents died, and when her only son entered a seminary, uninterested in conventional relations. She clung to it when my mother was raped by her own husband, and clung to it more ferociously still when my mother ran off with Father and then died a year later. The Archbishop of Sevilla, numerous priests, and convents had profited financially from her sorrows. But with the death of the little boy and the suicide of Rodrigo, coupled with the reemergence of her angry firstborn, who was triumphantly taking over her properties, she felt old and abandoned by God. She had been raised in great luxury to marry a grandee of Spain, to lead a life of elegant piety above the common folk. But where had it gotten her, she had asked me once. During this period of her life, when she should have been at her most comfortable and serene, she felt singled out as the object of some cruel celestial joke.

With Carlos often at court in Madrid, she wandered about her palatial home feeling like a stranger. When she did manage to pray, it was for an early death. At a particularly low point, she sought reconciliation with Doña Soledad, and received it. When my great-aunt saw the state Inmaculada had fallen into, she opened her arms and held her close until both were reduced to tears.

"What is to become of me?" my grandmother asked.

Despite Inmaculada's initial coldness toward them, Caitríona and Rosario were kind to her. They made a point of deferring to her, and she was humbled by it. Her spirits gradually improved. The relief she felt being back in Doña Soledad's good graces and the attention paid to her by the younger women were a balm. Her bitterness abated. Her once exacting standards eased.

With the arrival of spring, and with Carlos still in Madrid, Caitríona invited Inmaculada to Carmona, where she encouraged her mother-in-law to put the house back as she remembered it.

"But the estate is no longer mine," she said.

"I think it should be yours again," Caitríona replied. "And I will say as much to Carlos. We have too many houses as it is. I'm sure I can bring him around to it."

In mid-April Inmaculada received a letter from Carlos returning the property to her. In truth he had never been happy there. In his mind, the estate was a punishment meted out by his father.

One afternoon there, at the end of the month, shortly before returning to Sevilla, Caitríona and my grandmother sat in a room with a commanding view of the green fields that rippled from Carmona toward Marchena.

"Carlos has told me that you tend my daughter's grave," Inmaculada said.

"I do so whenever I can, madam," Caitríona replied, "at the behest of Doña Soledad."

"I was not a good mother to her," Inmaculada said. "As she got older, she resembled her father more in character than I, and he adored her. I tried as best I could. But it wasn't sufficient. It is another sin I try to atone for."

"Mothers and daughters," Caitríona said softly. "From what I have seen, it is rarely easy. Like fathers with sons."

"Did you get on with your mother?" Inmaculada asked.

"I did, by and large," Caitríona replied, "if only because her sons were so hateful to everyone. In comparison, I was a relief to her."

Caitríona told me that at this point, Inmaculada probably realized that it had been a mistake to bring up the topic of her mother. Soledad Medina had related the tale to Inmaculada concerning the terrible story of the woman's enslavement, and she saw the effect it had on Caitríona's countenance.

"I'm sure she would have loved you anyway," my grandmother said. "I only bring it up because you are close to the age Guada would have been, and you both loved the same man, and had a child with him, and now you are my daughter-in-law."

"Yes, madam."

"I feel closer to you than I did to her. That is the truth. I am ashamed to speak it."

Caitríona said that Inmaculada, still beautiful despite her wrinkles and graying hair, stared out at the fields more intensely then, filling the silence between them with tears. Caitríona put her own sad memories aside and reached out to her. Inmaculada took her hand and squeezed it without averting her eyes from the view. "Forgive me, child," she said. "Forgive me."

– XXII –

While Caitríona and Inmaculada were in Carmona, Rosario visited Doña Soledad to keep her company at the Casa de Pilatos in Sevilla. One day they sat in the shade, in the large rear garden, by a row of freshly trimmed boxwoods. Rosario's young son, Francisco, had fallen asleep on a large cushion beneath the branches of a lemon tree. The two women reminisced about the late Duke of Medina-Sidonia.

"I wanted to have a child by him," Doña Soledad said, studying the liver spots on her hands.

"I had no expectations," Rosario replied. "My first husband did all he could to get me pregnant, but nothing ever came of it. I assumed the fault was mine. And then when it happened with the duke, I worried because of his age, I worried that something might turn out wrong with the boy."

"Bah," Soledad said. "Men are like lions, lying around and rutting into old age if they can, while women perform all the dreary tasks. Even I, who had various households filled with servants, did infinitely more work than my husband, whose singular interest was whoring."

This made the both of them laugh.

Soledad Medina had been fair in her youth. She admired Rosario's dark beauty. She saw what the duke had been taken by and desired: the young woman's silken olive skin, the lustrous, long, coal-black hair, the white teeth and bright eyes, the smoothness and freshness of her.

"You mustn't be done with men so soon," the older woman said. "It would be a crime for beauty like yours to be wasted in a town as dull as Sanlúcar. You must stay here longer, and we can organize a ball with Caitríona and Inmaculada."

Years later, when we had grown close to each other, Rosario told me that as she entertained Doña Soledad's proposal that day, planning for a ball she very much doubted would ever take place, she considered the fact that this unexpected friendship with such an eminent woman, and the friendship that had blossomed between her and Caitríona, had come about as a direct result of Don Rodrigo's and the little boy's deaths. She looked at Doña Soledad and wondered how long she might live. She looked at her sleeping son, so young and beautiful. She said that life suddenly overwhelmed her at that moment. She pictured her bedchamber in Sanlúcar, sixty kilometers to the south of her, quiet and empty, the wide bed where her son was made, where the duke had died, where Doña Soledad had made love with the duke before Rosario was born, the Alpujarran rug on the floor beside it, the balcony overlooking the dunes.

The duke was buried in his grave. All that had been his life was over. My father too was gone, and my mother, in whose service Rosario had once worked. She looked once more at the old noblewoman, and then at her sleeping boy, and for some reason she recalled the horrific story the duke always repeated when he had too much to drink. How, to lighten the ships of his floundering invincible armada, the men were forced to drive the cavalry horses overboard into the sea off the coast of Ireland, horses that had once been foals in Spain, born from Arabian mares, just like she'd been born out of her mother. Rosario looked down at herself in that moment and wondered what would become of the dress she was wearing after she died. What would become of Francisco when he grew up, and how would he remember her?

She told me that after a short while Doña Soledad fell asleep in her chair. Her head was tilted to the side. A thin rivulet of spittle trailed down the noblewoman's soft, powdered chin. Rosario imagined the horses unable to reach the shore, submerged under the dark murky ocean, eyes wide with fright, their elegant legs still in motion.

– XXIII –

Though the relationship with my Uncle Carlos would begin badly, it improved over the years. By the time the tales I am chronicling here drew to a close, he moved to Italy. We try to see each other at least once a year. On one of those occasions, at his residence in Rome, he described his first audience at court in Madrid with King Philip IV.

He had not been to the capital since his early teens, since the dismal occasion when his father brought him to a brothel there. Don Rodrigo's foolish idea had been to try to make a man of his effeminate heir. Returning on his own almost twenty years later as an adult in all his finery, his inheritance secured, a married man of substance, he did his best to hide any evidence of provincialism. He allowed himself to be seduced by Madrid's pomp and circumstance, its elevated opinions of itself. He began to understand why his father had spent so much time there, a city where a man of his status had the world at his feet.

The king's closest advisor, the powerful Count-Duke of Olivares, received Carlos in an upper tower of the Alcázar Palace. The room was stark with a high ceiling. Spring light streamed in through tall windows. Olivares was posing for a portrait, standing as still as he could by a table covered with a thick red velvet cloth. The portraitist, handsome and smaller in stature, was working at a massive easel. The artist and his subject were friends, and were engaged in leisurely conversation when Carlos was announced. Olivares was a large, corpulent man with a small head who kept his hair short and mustache long. He was dressed in black for the occasion, mirroring the practice of Spanish royalty that embraced austerity and eschewed ostentation. But, unable perhaps to repress a vein of vanity, the count-duke's black tunic displayed a large red cross that identified him as a Knight of the Order of Santiago. Stuck into a leather belt and plainly visible as well was a large key identifying him as the king's *Sumiller de Corps*.

"Don Carlos," Olivares said in a loud baritone voice. "I do beg your pardon. You catch me *in flagrante*, a fly caught in the web of our esteemed countryman, Don Diego Velázquez."

Velázquez pointed his brush at the count-duke. "Do stay still, my friend."

"You see my predicament," Olivares said to Carlos without averting his gaze.

The artist approached my uncle and greeted him, offering him a chair from which he could observe both the canvas and the model. Carlos knew little about art; nevertheless he was impressed by the nearly completed canvas.

"What do you think?" Olivares asked. "The devil will not allow me to see it until it is done."

"It is most extraordinary," my uncle replied, trying to keep his voice deep and manly. "It looks more like you than you, my lord."

This caused the other two men to laugh, and Carlos was pleased.

"I wanted to meet with you and brief you before presenting you to His Majesty," Olivares said, getting down to business.

"I am at your absolute disposal, sir," Carlos replied, thinking a sentence like that to be most befitting. He too had dressed as somberly as his sense of style permitted. He remembered that day's wardrobe with precision: dark chocolate velvet breeches, black boots, and a deep burgundy coat with silver buttons, but with a lime-green silk lining he prayed would remain unseen.

"Are you much of a military man, Don Carlos?" Olivares asked. "I know a good part of your youth was spent—wisely I feel—as a scholar. But have you any martial aspirations?"

"I have not given it much thought, my lord."

"We are at war, you know."

"I do, sir, if only by way of the rising taxes levied upon my estates."

This too, he said, was the kind of thing he thought he should say, to bolster his self-regard, and to impress his listener.

"Precisely," Olivares said. "And I know you've an uncle who has been defending Spain in Flanders with high honor."

"My uncle Gonzalo."

"The very same," said the count-duke. "The siege of Wimpfen, the siege of Hochst, the siege of Heidelberg, all of them tremendously successful."

This Gonzalo relation was my grandfather's brother, and the governor of the Duchy of Milan. He was unmarried, a fighter and a loner from whom the wealthier and more colorful Don Rodrigo had stayed away.

"I would send you to join him, but he has retired and has been replaced by another man just as fierce and patriotic, Ambrosio Spinola, born like myself in Italy. His forces are gathering to lay siege on Breda."

"Sir."

"I am going to send you to stand at his side, or in the background if you prefer, away from arrows and cannon fire. But I feel a bit of military glory would be just the thing to impress the king."

Carlos was alarmed, but strove to hide it.

"And you are in need of an heir," the count-duke went on, "a proper heir of your own. As soon as you can present these two elements, the world here at court will be yours. You shall do me proud

105

as a fellow son of Sevilla, and you will be setting an example for those of your station afflicted with lesser ambition and laxer moral fiber."

My uncle told me he was horrified, but realized he could not refuse. Doing so would weaken his position. And he confessed that the adventure had its appeal: to be a soldier, armed and arrayed in dashing armor as an officer, standing side by side with other young men, swords raised on the faraway fields of Flanders.

"I shall be delighted, my lord," he said without any hesitation.

To reach the monarch they had to navigate many layers of the palace, traversing room after room, each one barer and more protected than the one before it, guards and servants bowing before them. By the time they arrived at the inner sanctum, where the king awaited, Carlos was in precisely the state of awe the baroque protocol was designed to inspire. His first view of the monarch was in profile. The great-grandson of the Emperor Carlos V was kneeling in prayer at a prie-dieu before a stark wooden cross, affixed to an otherwise bare wall. He was hatless, and what first drew my uncle's attention was the monarch's wavy red hair and light orange beard, followed in quick succession by his distinctive nose and prominent chin. He said that seen from the side like that, the royal visage resembled a quarter moon.

Olivares kept his head bowed until the king made the sign of the cross, stood, and faced them. Carlos then saw that the monarch was much closer to him in age than the older count-duke. The king ignored Olivares and addressed Carlos directly. He did not smile. Employing the royal first person plural, he spoke as if enclosed within an aura of gloom. Carlos remembered thinking that the king had married the thirteen-year-old daughter of Marie de Medici and King Henry IV of France, and he wondered what the marriage might be like.

"We were grieved to learn of your father's death," said the king.

"Your Majesty."

"He was close to my father, and always kind to me."

"Your Majesty."

"We take it you did not get along with him."

"His devotion to the crown was such," Carlos replied, "that there was little left for his children."

"We take it you studied for the priesthood."

"Yes, Your Majesty."

"Most admirable. With the passing of my father, a new age is upon us, one we wish to count upon you for, to aid in our endeavor to restore dignity and decorum to the houses of nobility."

"I shall apply myself to this endeavor with heart and soul, Your Majesty."

"We are pleased, and pleased as well for the service you shall render us in the Low Countries."

"Your Majesty."

Carlos was astonished. He saw that his fate as a soldier for the crown had been decided before Olivares even spoke to him. He was irritated but impressed, and relieved that he had answered the call as he did. Then, in the very next moment, he was more astonished still.

"We look forward to the birth of your heir," the king went on, "so that your house might continue to share in the glory of our enterprise."

What did they know? Carlos wondered. The intrusiveness of the audience came as a shock. It was too reminiscent of what his life had been like in the seminary. While maintaining a brave face, he resolved to go out on the town that evening and do as he pleased, if only to prove that he could.

The king left the room without a smile or the utterance of another word. Carlos and Olivares retraced their path in silence as well, until they came into the vast entrance hall that was populated with many people rushing to and fro.

"Is he always like that?" my uncle asked.

"He takes his vocation very seriously," Olivares replied.

But, Carlos told me, everyone knew that Philip IV was trained and schooled by Olivares himself.

***

He went to Flanders. He took part in the siege of Breda. He got along well with Ambrosio Spinola. He witnessed much death and destruction, and for the first time in his life, he fell in love. The object of his passion was a young nobleman called Hermenegildo Van der Wyden. He was blond like my uncle, of German extraction, and from Granada. Given all the woe this gentleman caused me, my uncle apologized once again for this relationship, but then added, "You, yourself, though much younger than I, may have already taken note of the fact that in matters of the heart, we have no control."

With the siege of Breda successfully concluded, Carlos returned to Spain bedecked with honors and accompanied by Hermenegildo. When he rejoined Caitríona in Sevilla, over eight months had passed since the couple had seen each other. She told me she noticed the change in him at once. He was broader and more handsome, more serious. He had taken on a gait and posture and a set of facial expressions that were modeled, ironically, or so she imagined, after his own deceased father. She did not hesitate to say as much aloud to him, and to her relief the comment amused and even seemed to please him.

"War alters a man," he said to her, though I suspect he had not once unsheathed his sword in battle. "And passion," he added.

"Passion?" she asked, raising an eyebrow. "A he or a she?"

"The former my dear, not to fear."

"So not everything has changed."

"No."

"I'm glad for it," she said.

"But we're to make an heir, Caitríona," he said. "The king has all but commanded it."

"What an odd thing for a king, or anyone, to command," she replied, "especially in light of the fact that you already have an heir in my son."

"I have given this careful consideration," he said, "and I can assure you, in writing if you wish, that Patrick's fortune and future shall not in any way be diminished. But if you could produce another boy, for me, it would bode well for all of us."

"To have it in writing will suit me fine," she said.

***

Later in our lives, when Caitríona felt sufficiently separated from those days, she confessed to me that the only man she had been with until then was my father, and that she had wondered from time to time if the pleasure she recalled was inherent in the act itself, or dependent on one's partner. When the agreed-upon evening arrived, she drank many goblets of wine, determined to go through with it. Bathed in candle glow, Carlos asked her to lie upon their bed, on her stomach. He instructed her to raise her chemise, just above her hips. Then they were joined by Hermenegildo, who proceeded to embrace Carlos. When my uncle was sufficiently aroused, he turned from his German lover and mounted her. Caitríona felt discomfort, and little else. Nine months later, she gave birth to a baby girl.

– PART FOUR –

PART FOUR

– XXIV –

The Pacific swelled and swerved. Furious, freezing winds blew. The food was abominable. The ship was small and primitive, the sailors taciturn. For many days I was ill. Father held my hand and did his best to distract me. I despaired and cried to go home, aiming much venom at him and blaming him for our exile and misfortune.

But then the sea becalmed and my appetite returned. I marveled at the families of whales, and at the vast schools of tuna that often raced through the water at either side of us. At night the stars were clearer and closer than any I had seen. The sailors sang plaintive melodies and taught me how to tie knots and gut fish. Land appeared, a chain of mysterious islands encircled by herds of seals, then more ocean and milder temperatures. Finally, a vast coastline emerged from a thick morning mist. We sailed down alongside of it. By the time we reached the immense harbor, where the Ezochi colony was hidden, I was more at home at sea than on land.

Father stepped off the ship in his samurai garb, and I behind him, in a blue silk kimono decorated with flying cranes. We were regarded with bulging eyes and open mouths. It was difficult to know whether they saw us as gods or fools. The natives lived in simple huts and wore little clothing. At night some of the men danced, and chanted to spirits in rooms dug underground that were covered with branches. The Ezochi colonists dressed like Japanese farmers. They had built themselves more sophisticated abodes. Four of the colonists had children with some of the native women.

The sailors who brought us there remained for a week. A few of them stayed behind at the colony, but most returned. I would be lying if I did not reveal the distress I experienced at seeing the ship sail away. It was heading back to the land that was my home, a land of comfort and order and civilization, where I had been raised and treated like a princess. In the primitive place and crude conditions in which we found ourselves, a place whose geographical reality I barely comprehended, Father seemed rejuvenated—freed, stronger, alive, and curious—while I felt abandoned and surrounded by filth.

***

Life in the colony was so slovenly that I was greatly relieved when Father informed me it was time for us to move on. After discussing a route with the Ezochi men and using sign language with the natives that included much tracing of maps in the earth with pointed sticks, we set out early one morning on foot.

For two weeks we made our way south and then inland, through a warm and fertile valley. Sometimes we passed native settlements where we were fed and treated kindly. Most of the time we were in the wild. We carried our swords. Father had his bow and a quiver filled with arrows slung over one shoulder. Over the other he carried a sack containing our keepsakes and better clothing. We wore simple trousers and tunics. When our sandals gave out, we traded two arrows for short deerskin boots like the natives wore. In the wild we grilled fish and hares. Once we tried cooking a snake that Father beheaded. It made us both violently ill. Guarding our modesty, we took turns bathing in rivers and streams. When Father saw the way some of the native men were looking at me, he cut my hair short to make me look like a boy. At first I cried, but after a time I liked it.

I forgot my sorrows. What occupied my waking hours was the beauty of the landscape and the daily challenges we faced to remain healthy and alive. At night we conversed by the fire. He told me stories about my mother, and my great-aunt, stories about Sevilla. I could only speak to him of what I knew, of what we had left behind in Japan. It was on one of these nights that he told me that his real father had come from China, and that this knowledge made him feel freer. He told me I might have a brother or sister somewhere, in Europe. From then on, we both wondered about Caitríona, though I could barely remember her. Sometimes in the night I could hear him pleasuring himself, and sometimes, when I knew he was asleep, I would do the same.

At a campsite near a canyon, by a narrow river with a small sandy beach, a waterfall, shade from trees, and smooth flat boulders to sleep upon, I was stung by a large red insect. The pain was terrible, my leg became swollen, and a fever gripped me. Though he tried not to show it, Father was desperate. A native family came by and gave me some tree bark to chew on, and within a few days I recovered. Father told me the site reminded him of the place on the island of Paxos, where he and Caitríona and I had lived for a summer in Greece after the shipwreck. My memories of that place were only brief flashes of sea and light, and a vision of their bodies together. I saw that the recollection filled him with melancholy, and for the first time I realized how fleeting his romances had been. He had only been with my mother for a year before she died. He had been with Caitríona for less than that. Though he lived with Yokiko for almost seven years, their relationship had not been blessed with passion.

***

We crossed a desert and learned to savor cactus fruit. Where the desert ended, green plains descended to a river. We followed the river north, content to be close to water. Sometimes there were clear pools that had formed along the river's course, where we bathed and swam. We stayed with the river and went through a canyon so vast, so deep, and so foreign in its aspect, that we feared we might be approaching an entrance to hell. After three days the river narrowed and spilled into a lake, and on the shore of the lake we found the remains of a settlement. Wooden crosses were stuck in the ground with names etched into them. All of the names were Spanish. The largest cross bore the name of Hernando de Alarcón. "Does this mean that Spain is near?" I asked.

"No," Father said, smiling at my ignorance. "It means the Spanish have come far."

Three wide skiffs pulled onto the shore had succumbed to time. The hulls were old and cracked, the oars splintered or broken. I went into a wood to collect additional kindling for the evening's fire and found a small herd of horses. Father chose three of them and decided they were offspring from the horses the Spanish had brought. He spent some days taming them, and we used old blankets left behind for saddles on two of the mares and kept the third to carry our belongings. Then we set out, continuing due east.

We fled Japan because Father wished for me to have a better life. I also believe he was driven by a desire to return to the place where he had become his own man, where he fell in love with someone as foreign and exotic to him as he was to her, where he had acquired an independence unavailable to him in Sendai. It was something I could understand. But what of these men, these Spaniards who had traveled so far from their home, only to end up at the shore of a lake in the middle of nowhere? What had driven them? I suppose all inhabited lands began with men like these, but what incited them to wander so? Poverty? The promise of glory and riches? An inner emptiness of some kind, a refusal of domestic comfort that might be considered manly, but which might really be something else? No other animal I knew of—though I knew very little—was wont to roam so far from home. But then, as we rode through that virgin country, rampant with plains, mountains, and russet plateaus, I thought, what is home, really?

***

A week later, we rode into a large settlement that took us by surprise. Many natives from a tribe called Zuni lived there under the rule of Spanish soldiers and priests. The settlement even had a Spanish governor. Father told our story to this man, who was called Francisco de la Mora. He was astonished by our tale, though he seemed more interested in the harbor where the Ezochi colony was, and in the route we had taken to get there from Japan. For years the Spaniards had been looking for the mythical "Cities of Cibola," thought to be filled with gold—gold for them to plunder, just as the priests only cared about converting the natives, be they the natives of that land so new to us or inhabitants of Japan.

To keep his promise to the Ezochi elder, Father lied about the location of the colony. He informed the priests in the settlement that both of us had been baptized, he in Mexico and I in Spain. He told me to pretend to be a good Christian, so that they would leave us alone. I had little idea about what that meant, and so he had to teach me. The settlement had existed for many centuries before the Spanish arrived, when Zuni natives lived without need of any name more complicated than "Ogapoge." The invaders "christened" it with the absurd name of La Villa Real de la Santa Fe de San Francisco de Asís—The Royal Town of the Holy Faith of Saint Francis of Assisi. The soldiers stationed there simply called it Santa Fe.

We remained there longer than we should have. Father was trying to obtain a letter of passage from the governor, so that we might travel south through Mexico in the hope of finding a ship from

117

Veracruz bound for Spain. After almost a week had passed, the soldier in command of the garrison told the governor he was uncomfortable with Father having his unusual swords so in view at all hours
of the day, especially since he was a foreigner who looked more Zuni
than Christian. They asked that his swords be confiscated. The governor agreed. Father refused. Despite his letter, now old and parched,
from King Philip III, which instructed all subjects of Spain to give
Father special treatment, the governor sided with his soldiers. Father
was seized and put into a primitive jail with some of the natives,
Zuni tribesmen who were protesting taxes the governor had begun
to levy on them. They assumed I posed no threat and left me alone.

Troubled, suspicious, and alone, I left the settlement and repaired
to the hills. Much of the landscape was dry and dusty with impressive
canyons and rock formations, but there were streams and a river
where grass and trees grew. I set up camp, fished and hunted. Zuni
women came and did their wash. I did my best to learn the rudi-
ments of their language. Often in the early evening, with no one else
about, I would bathe. On one of those occasions a Zuni warrior, a
handsome young man named Lonan, spied on me and saw I was a
girl. He came down to the shore and strode into the shallows. He
called out to me. I told him to go away in every language I knew. But
he only laughed and came closer. He tried to force himself on me.
Naked and without a weapon, I used *atemi* on him, and subdued
him. Alerted by the noise, other warriors and Zuni women came and
witnessed this, and much was made of it. Lonan was angry and
humiliated. Each time I let him up he tried again to overpower me.
Each time I brought him down. Finally, he desisted, unable to rise. I
dressed and came back over to him. By then the others had come
closer. I helped him up. All of them looked at me in a new way.

With the little of their language that I learned, and using my
hands, I asked them to help me free Father from the jail. Some days

later, on the afternoon of the night we would sneak into the settlement, Lonan approached me and gave me a bracelet made of leather and beads. It was an offering of respect that spoke well of him. Unsure if we would survive the assault on the jail, I decided to go with him on his horse to the river, and there I gave myself to him. The encounter was brief and rough, and hurt more than anything else, but I was glad to have done it.

Just before dawn, we snuck into the settlement. I held my short sword against the throat of the guard. I told him to let Father and the others go. When he tried to grab me, I stabbed him in the heart. The blade went in between his ribs, just as I had been taught, and I saw life go out of him. The others came in behind me, and we freed Father and the Zunis that were imprisoned with him. Father recovered his weapons. Then more soldiers appeared, and we had to face them. Father and I, fighting back to back, slayed six of them before we were able to escape. Lonan was run through with a Spanish sword and died on the spot. I killed and beheaded the man that did it. The Spaniards at the jail were the first men I ever killed in active battle. The natives we freed marveled to see us decimate their oppressors. We rode away on Zuni horses. We galloped deep into the countryside. Once we were safe, I began to shake, and Father consoled me and expressed his pride in my skill and courage. The Zunis agreed and took us to a large cave, and they sang to me. The Zuni believe that their dead become rainmakers, and that rather than rising into the heavens, their spirits reside below a sacred lake, in a region they call *ko'luwala*. I prayed that Lonan was there and that he would not forget me.

– XXV –

After what happened at the settlement of Santa Fe, our route to Spain by way of Mexico was closed to us. We embarked upon a journey much longer than Father had ever imagined. The Ezochi map, shown to us before we left Japan, was only accurate at its westernmost edge. The land we came to, and needed to cross, was immensely vast. The North American continent was enormous and varied, populated with many native tribes. Most of them were friendly to us, some of them less so. We crossed flat plains for days on end, and then a region of lowlands for weeks, coming to a mighty river. Father decided to cross the river rather than take it south, for he feared it might bring us too close to other Spanish settlements.

We crossed the river on a raft that took us two weeks to build. Even so, one of the horses bolted rather than get on board and ran away. Autumn arrived, and as we started to climb into highlands, the snows came. We spent the winter moving through mountains. We almost perished. We wrapped ourselves in animal furs. We broke through ice-covered ponds and lakes to fish for sustenance. The two remaining mares grew thin. I thought about Lonan, my Zuni samurai, and wondered how my life would have been had I stayed with his tribe. I dreamed about him, and mourned him, and never said a word to Father about him.

With spring came rains and mud. During all of this time Father kept cutting my hair and kept shaving, and we continued to bathe, remaining faithful to our Japanese customs. We kept our tattered clothes clean. We kept our swords and minds sharp. As we descended from the mountains onto a coastal plain, we met more and more settlers who had come to America from northern Europe. All of them were filled with wonder at our story, for none had been as far west as we.

They spoke to us of a great port to the north, where many ships came and went, crossing the Atlantic. By the time we got there and saw the narrow island of New Amsterdam, we looked like Zuni renegades, wearing the clothing the native tribes wore, skins and moccasins and fur capes. The only things we retained from Japan were our weapons and the sack where my kimonos and Father's samurai clothes remained folded and almost forgotten.

We set the horses free in a meadow. I cried at leaving them, and prayed the days left to them might be peaceful. We reached the island colony by canoe. The Dutch had purchased the isle from natives nine years earlier. The settlement was concentrated at the southern end, where a fort was being built. Most of the inhabitants, some three hundred people, were men from Antwerp and Rotterdam. As those we passed and spoke with began to discern we were neither natives nor fur traders, despite our garb and appearance, we were directed to a building that housed the Dutch West India Company. From the porch of this building I saw a tall and imposing ship moored in the bay.

Though it was still morning, the man in charge of the office appeared to be drunk. He was short and rotund and dressed in black. The more that Father expressed a desire to book passage on the handsome ship that would soon sail for Europe, the more the man insisted we remain and settle there. A Christian preacher arrived and interrupted the conversation. He viewed us with suspicion. I heard the word "pagan" bandied about. This man too seemed to be inebriated. Just as Father and I began to despair and look for a way to escape, a miracle occurred that justified all of the hardships and the thousands of kilometers we had traveled since leaving Japan.

A tall and handsome man, cold sober, entered the room. He had broad shoulders, and a broken nose, and wore the clean navy uniform of a ship's captain. He and Father stared at each other. To the astonishment and displeasure of the other two gentlemen, this captain strode over and wrapped his arms about Father's shoulders, declaring loudly, "I cannot believe it! What in the devil's name are you doing in this godforsaken place?"

"Captain," was all Father said.

"Good grief, man!" cried Kurt the Dutchman. "How is it possible?"

"You know each other?" the preacher interjected, belaboring the obvious.

"Do we know each other?" the captain replied. "We were shipmates in the Indian Ocean, shipmates in Japan. This man, gentlemen, is a samurai and a prince, a figure of ancient royalty."

Father hardly looked princely that day, but the other two gave him a second appraisal. He had lines etched in his face by then, and gray in his hair. He was slimmer than ever, dressed head to toe like one of the Indians the Dutch settlers regarded so warily.

"And who might you be, young man?" the captain asked, looking at me.

"You've actually met before," Father said with a grin.

"I do not think so, Shiro-san."

"I shall give you a hint," Father said. "The young man is in fact a young lady."

"No! Can it be?"

"It is."

I bowed to him like a proper young woman from Sendai.

***

After much discussion and wrangling among the three westerners, Captain Kurt Vanderhooven ushered us out of the building and accompanied us in a skiff directly to his ship.

"We do not sail for another four days, but you'll be safer and more comfortable onboard. With nightfall, the island can turn dangerously rowdy."

We were introduced to the head mates and shown to our quarters, a handsome cabin for Father and one almost as nice for myself. Then we joined the captain on deck, for Father was eager to speak with him.

"I fear I am in debt to you, captain," Father said. "The gold you gave me, that allowed us to reach Sendai, shall be repaid in full upon our arrival in Spain."

"You, in debt to me?" the captain asked with what appeared to be genuine incredulity.

Father bowed.

"But it is I who am indebted to you, Shiro-san," the captain said, "more than you can ever know. This ship is mine and there are five more like it. I have homes in Amsterdam and Paris. The reason you see me here at all is thanks to you. Thanks to you I was able to leave the service in the Orient and come on as a major shareholder, to create my own routes and business."

Father was surprised.

"Was it the shogun?" he asked.

"Damn well right it was the shogun," said Kurt. "Whatever you asked of him and said to him benefited me a hundredfold. Less than a month after you left Hirado, just as I was about to abandon hope and be on my way, messengers arrived from Edo offering me exclusive trade agreements that have made me a very rich man indeed. It is I who am indebted to you. I promised myself that were I ever to sce you again, I would show my deepest gratitude, and here you are, come out of the woods like a wild man on the other side of the Earth."

Though I never expressed it to anyone, the first thing I thought upon hearing this was that if Father's influence with the shogun was such that it made this towering man so wealthy, then surely if he had gone to the shogun about the problem we were having with Date Tadamune, it would have been solved. Yokiko might still be alive; my grandmother would not have poisoned her and retired to a monastery; I would never have had to leave Japan. Father's stubbornness, his discretion, his unwillingness to risk damaging the reputation of Date Masamune had taken me away from all that I had known, had dragged me across seas and across a land so vast and wild, it was yet another miracle to have survived it.

On the other hand, there I was, a young woman of sixteen who had been more places than most people see in three lifetimes. I had learned to fight like a samurai. I had killed men, ridden horses, skinned deer, known natives of all description, swum in lakes, rivers, and two seas. I had known a man. I spoke four languages. I was my father's daughter.

– XXVI –

From the day we came on board his ship, its every surface scrubbed and polished, we put our deerskins away. Staring the island of *Manna-hata,* at the pristine woods north of the ale-soaked Dutch settlement, I adjusted my kimono. I wrapped and tied my obi as Mizuki and Yokiko had taught me. I decided to let my hair grow. I returned to sleeping on a mattress with proper bedcovers. Most of this process was a pleasurable relief, but some of it I resented. Perhaps resentment is too strong a word. The experience of crossing the great North American continent had changed me. It made me self-reliant, and it brought about some habits that will last for the rest of my life. From then on, I would always favor the simplest sort of clothing. I would always sleep with a window open, regardless of the season. And I would always be impatient with courtly manners.

Though larger and more advanced, the Dutch settlement of New Amsterdam we were about to leave reminded me in many ways of the Ezochi colony nestled in that other natural harbor facing the Pacific. We arrived at the latter from Japan. We were about to depart for Europe from the former. Neither place gave me any impression it might survive for long, built too precariously at the edges of a massive continent that was sparsely inhabited with sundry tribes and wild game. Japan and China and India were deep, sophisticated civilizations. Spain and Italy, England and Holland, also had claims to serious advancement, manners, and knowledge. But I thought that the savage continent we had traversed would remain that way: primitive, unconquerable, unruly, a gift from nature far more precious than the illusory gold that brought so many barbarians to its shores.

∗∗∗

The voyage to Rotterdam across the North Atlantic was calm. Our meals were prepared by a cook and served at a table with French wines poured from crystal decanters. Kurt tutored me in the proper use of knives, forks, and spoons—skills Father was amused to see me learn, but which he had no interest in. One day, taking a promenade on deck, Kurt recalled the first day he saw me.

"How small your hands were," he said.

He took my hand in his own, large and bony. It caught me unawares.

"As you can see, they are still small," I said, because it was true and because I sensed it was what he wished to think. He had no idea of the variety of lethal weapons they had held, what my hands had done to wild game and to some people during the previous two years.

"I shall never forget the gruesome scene that confronted me as I stepped aboard that wretched ship in the Indian Ocean," he said, "the butchered bodies strewn upon the foredeck, and you asleep in your father's arms up by the helm, your little kimono splattered with blood. And now, here you are walking next to me, a grown woman on the other side of the world."

Upon landing, we accompanied him to Amsterdam and stayed at his home. He lived there when he could, with his wife and three boys. The four-story brick structure faced a canal. Its interior, narrow and very clean, boasted Asian screens and tapestries, thick silk curtains and Italian carpets. His wife, somewhat stout with red cheeks, was quiet, close to him in age. The boys, like their father, were blond and shy. All of them were kind to me. His wife treated me to dresses she had to alter and chemises made in Paris, to all manner of undergarments I was not used to, plus hosiery and shoes.

I was grateful and wore them for a time in order to please her, but I still preferred my Japanese robes and sandals. I was in no hurry to embrace the European half of me that Father insisted I had, but which I did not feel in the least. It was plain that Kurt fancied me. He had tried to hide it on the voyage across the North Atlantic, but one evening at his home in Amsterdam, when a young painter friend of his came to dinner and paid me great favor, it was difficult for our host to hide his annoyance, something Father and Kurt's wife later commented on later with great amusement.

Despite the chasm of years between us, I grew fond of him, this tall and rugged man who had brought me safely to Japan as a small girl, and who was now bringing me back to Spain as a woman. His company was always welcome and instructive, his generosity genuine and unencumbered. Back then, his thirst for commerce still outweighed any pleasure he derived from social intercourse. He had another impending voyage of trade, this time to the Caribbean, and the idea of losing sight of him saddened me. He was going to take us to Spain on his way to the West Indies. Our last night in Amsterdam, before setting off to Rotterdam again where the ship awaited us, was my seventeenth birthday. Kurt took me aside, away from his family, and made me the gift of a pearl necklace with a diamond clasp.

"You should wear this often," he said, fastening it about my neck. "The more you wear them, the brighter they will shine. And perhaps it's time for you to put away those primitive bracelets about your wrist."

These "primitive" bracelets were the three given to me by my Sendai masters, and the beaded leather one given to me by Lonan. I declined his suggestion. But feeling Kurt's fingertips on the nape of my neck as he fastened the diamond clasp provoked a shock of pleasure that my lover in the mountains of Santa Fe had not. It descended through my body, surprising me, jolting me, telling me something.

Kurt was twice my age. During the crossing from New Amsterdam, it was his shyness that appealed to me. He was the very opposite of Lonan. He treated me with care, with delicacy, but not in a way that diminished his masculinity. The magnetism of attraction was in the air between us. I often had the sensation that rather than express what he truly felt, he would speak instead of almost anything else. I knew it, and he knew it, and I appreciated it. He respected me. He respected Father. He respected his wife and family. The feelings he was hiding were a source of turmoil to him.

***

The voyage from Rotterdam to Brest was rough. I was as seasick as I had been during the first weeks aboard the ship with the Ezochi fishermen after leaving Japan. Kurt held me as I vomited over the side. Father, impervious to the high seas, placed cool damp cloths upon my forehead; sitting by my berth at night, he sang me Sendai lullabies. After Brest, the weather was beautiful, the Atlantic calm. As days of sun and cool breezes passed, I saw my life as one of constant displacement. We had been traveling for two years. Sendai, so fundamental to my identity, was beginning to feel like something I had dreamed, something I could only half remember upon waking. The world was a borderless orb we moved about like the Bedouins. Given my youth, I found it invigorating. But Father was exhausted, and swore that upon landing at our destination, he would never set foot on another ship.

Back in command of his vessel, far from his family and the ties of country, Kurt relaxed and spent much time with me. Had it not been for the presence of Father and the crew, who knows what might have transpired between us? He had kind, sad eyes, broad shoulders, and that broken nose. We traded stories about our youth. His had taken place in Amsterdam, and then on the high seas in the Pacific. He had sailed with a mad captain named Jan Pieterszoon Coen. It was Coen who unleashed a massacre upon the inhabitants of the Banda Islands where, with the aid of Japanese mercenaries, thousands of people lost their lives, tortured and beheaded. Kurt's involvement, what he witnessed and what he did, changed him. Afterward he managed to get his own commission and decided to dedicate his professional life to the improvement of relations between his own countrymen and the inhabitants of the islands they traded with. His attitude caused him to be ostracized and made fun of by numerous officials of the Dutch East India organization, but his gift for trade and the loyalty he inspired in his crews had prevented his being relieved from duty. I told him about Mizuki and Yokiko and Nobuko. I told him about Date Masamune and Date Tadamune. I spoke to him in vague terms about my training. I did my best to describe North America, while omitting certain events.

After the evening meal we would stroll on deck. Father accompanied us. The tension in the air was palpable, frustrating, pleasurable. Kurt would point out different constellations and relate them to Greek mythology, and Father and I would describe how the heavens were considered in Japan. Sometimes Kurt would try to speak in Japanese and I would laugh, and Father would chide me. In bed, alone, listening to the creaking rigging and feeling the gentle swell of the sea, I would imagine him coming to me in the middle of the night. I would roll the pearls of the necklace he gave me with my fingers, wondering what, if anything, might happen between us; wondering about where I was heading, to the land of a mother I never knew.

On our last night, somewhere between Lisbon and the coast of Spain, as our stroll concluded, Father did something unusual. He bid us goodnight and left us alone on deck, save for the helmsman and a sailor or two. We found a corner where no one could see us. I embraced him fiercely, surprising him. I buried my face against his breast. I breathed in the scent of him, a scent tinged with wine and tobacco, and the salt of the sea held within the weave of his damp coat. I felt his powerful arms around me, so different from my father's. I felt his hands clasping me through the thin material of my kimono.

"How slight you are," he whispered.

I looked up at him, barely able to see his eyes in the darkness.

And then he kissed me.

My first kiss.

Lonan had never kissed me.

It was such an intimate thing.

"Do you care for me, Masako?" he said.

"Yes," I said.

"I'm embarrassed." he said,

"Why are you embarrassed?" I asked.

"Because I am in love with you. I am embarrassed and I am miserable," he said. "I am so much older than you. I am married, with children. I sail the seas for a living. Tomorrow I shall put you ashore and perhaps never see you again."

We stood there by the railing clinging to each other in silence. We contemplated the truth of what he said, a truth I had thought of night after night.

"I care for you without embarrassment," I finally said to him. "I owe my life to you from long ago. You must find a way to return to me."

– XXVII –

Sanlúcar de Barrameda came into view the following morning. Gentle, early autumn light enveloped the ship. Father, Kurt, and I stood by the prow, observing the low dunes along the coast, the calm of the estuary, the blue winged magpies crossing overhead.

"When I first came here, I was a year older than you are now," Father said to me in Japanese. "After our ship docked, the samurais followed Hasekura Tsunenaga off the ship. There was much ceremony, trumpets and priests, and a line of brightly painted coaches waiting to take our delegation to a reception."

Hearing Father speaking to me in our language, Kurt backed away, respectfully, so as not to intrude. I looked at him with gratitude. He smiled, bowed, and turned. Father continued.

"Our needs were seen to by the Duke of Medina-Sidonia, represented that day by a man I killed two years later in front of the king of Spain. But on that first night, I stayed behind. I did not leave the ship. My relations with Hasekura Tsunenaga were not good then, and I was eager for peace. One more night aboard, after so many at sea crammed with other men, seemed a fair price to pay for the quiet and privacy it afforded me. I had the ship to myself. I climbed to the crow's nest in the darkness and listened to the gaiety going on in town. In the morning, I dove into these waters and swam, content, and feeling strangely at home. Later, I was chosen to ride to the duke's estate, deep in the countryside, to deliver a gift of thanks from Hasekura Tsunenaga. If I had not been chosen to go and meet the duke, I would never have met your mother, who was staying with him. You would not have been born. We would not be here now."

He was trembling. I took his hand.

"Fifteen years ago," Father continued, "you and I left Spain from here. I held you in my arms, wrapped in a scarf belonging to your mother. And now I am bringing you back. I am bringing you back as I promised."

As I held Father's hand, I realized for the first time, physically, in my body, that we were at our journey's end. We had been traveling for so long that I had taken this last trip in stride, adapting myself to another of what felt like an unending series of voyages. But after Father spoke, I confronted the fact that the estuary we were sailing through, the dunes on either side, the gentle land spreading out and gradually rising up into green hills and gray mountains, was Andalucia, my mother's land, a part of me I was seeing for the first time.

Father had come here as a young samurai all the way from Japan. Then he had striven against great adversity to bring me to Sendai so that I might have a Japanese childhood. Now he had taken me all the way back, back to where I came from. Tears fell from my eyes. How he must have loved her, I thought, to have cared for me as well as he did.

Spain and the Low Countries were technically at war during those years, and thus Kurt only stayed long enough to see us off. Father hugged him goodbye, something I had never seen him do before. I lingered behind to have a moment alone. I raised my left arm.

"On this wrist are the bracelets given me by my teachers and a dear friend, bracelets I shall never relinquish because they remind me of who I am."

Then I touched the pearls about my neck.

"These, no matter what happens, shall only be removed from my neck by you."

He took my hand, bowed, and kissed it. Once again, the sensation of his fingers upon my skin sent a shiver through me.

We waved goodbye from the wharf until the ship came about and went on its way, leaving Father and me alone. We stood with our swords, dressed in traditional Japanese clothing. The sun shone. The air was fresh and limpid. We loitered by my travel trunk that was packed with the clothing given to me in Amsterdam. We waited for someone, anyone, to appear. Thinking—erroneously, of course, but not knowing any better—that this small seaside town was to be my final destination, I was dismayed. Father, who knew better and who might have reassured me had I said something, appeared to be calm and relieved.

The smell of baking bread wafted down from a street close to the wharf. There, it mixed with a heavier but pleasant scent that surrounded a cavernous warehouse across from us. We peered into it and saw oaken barrels filled with Manzanilla wine, stored there for export. Father knocked on a door or two until an old woman, who remembered the arrival of the samurai delegation eighteen years earlier, began to speak with him in a most animated fashion. She wore a black shawl that she used to cover her mouth, as if embarrassed, a pose in direct contradiction with her loquacious manner. She asked us in after sending a young nephew up into the town to fetch us transport. Her house was humble, whitewashed, and damp. But bright light came in through a rear patio, where flowers grew, and a pair of hens pecked about.

The woman's good humor—I believe her name was Dolores—was matched only by the trove of misinformation she showered upon us. She served cool water from a clay jug, a *botijo*. And she offered us biscuits that were dense with anise seeds, and then a sticky, sweet wine that was difficult to swallow, but impossible to refuse, so as not to appear ungrateful. Father quickly deduced that the best tactic with such a personage consisted of keeping information about our travels and identities to a minimum, allowing her to compensate the vacuum thus created—and compensate she did. I was struck by her assumption that we spoke her language, and considering the fact that not a single woman had accompanied the original Japanese delegation in 1614, her lack of interest in me, and in my wardrobe, was curious as well. I write this after many years of living in Europe, but at the time I both looked and behaved like a seventeen-year-old Japanese woman from Sendai, albeit one who had known adventures unthinkable for most people, man or woman. In fact, to the best of my knowledge, I was the first adult Japanese woman to set foot in Europe.

Dolores' pronouncements concerning local gossip, internecine rivalries, land disputes, jealousies, recent crop failures, and vineyard swindles were possibly reliable. But in order perhaps to honor our status as visitors, as foreigners, she felt obliged to expatiate on matters wider afield. She confused north with south, east with west, kings with dukes and counts. She spoke of the Berbers, long driven from Spain, as if the caliphates of Córdoba and Granada had never been conquered, and were still hell-bent on cutting every Christian's head off. Her answer to the only important question Father put to her almost caused us to change our plans.

"I believe the late Duke of Medina-Sidonia keeps some fine houses nearby," he said to her, after taking the smallest possible sip of the wine.

"They've been closed and boarded up for years," she replied with an odd sparkle in her eyes. "The ghost of the duke haunts their halls and salons, you see, a ghost that howls with rage. No one could bear to live in them any longer."

"Rage at what?" I asked, unable to restrain myself.

"At how his oldest son took everything, cutting out all the other siblings and relatives, reducing them to paupers like the rest of us. Some have become shepherds, others have gone off to convents and seminaries."

Father considered the option of setting off directly for Sevilla— yet another journey. But when a cart appeared, drawn by a handsome mule and driven by a thin little old man in rope-soled sandals, permitting us to extricate ourselves from Dolores' domain, Father insisted on showing me the Medina-Sidonia house anyway. It was where he had recovered from wounds many years earlier, after being mauled in Sevilla and left for dead by my mother's husband and his guards. The grand house had been his sanctuary.

As the cart made its way up along the narrow streets of the village, there were hardly any people about, for it was the hour of the siesta. It enabled us to make our way through the town without drawing attention. Father trusted that after viewing the house, if only from the outside, we would be able to leave Sanlúcar before the ebullient Dolores had time to tell everyone about the latest visitors from the Orient.

The residence we approached was not the main Medina-Sidonia palace, but a more modest property just outside the town, regal and deceptively unadorned. It faced the dunes and the water and was protected by high, whitewashed walls that hid a large and beautiful Moorish garden. Recalling what Dolores had said, I asked Father if he believed in ghosts.

"No," he replied.

"But in Japan everyone believes in the *yūrei*," I said, "the souls of the dead that seek revenge."

"I am not one of them," he said, and asked the driver to stop.

"Both Yokiko and Nobuko believed in them," I said, "even Mizuki."

"And half of my fellow samurai," he said, looking at me, taking my hand and helping me down from the cart. "Do you think that mice have spirits, or dogs, or monkeys, or spiders?"

"Maybe," I said.

"Think about it," he said. "How likely is it?"

"Perhaps not very," I conceded.

"Precisely," he said. "When you step on a spider, when mice drown in a river, when monkeys slip from trees, they die, they rot like fallen fruit, they return into the earth, and that is the end of it. It is the same with us, I'm afraid."

"But maybe you are wrong," I said, somewhat irritated by his air of certainty.

"Maybe," he said, "but I doubt it."

Changing to Spanish, I queried the driver. "Tell me sir, do you believe in ghosts?"

He made the sign of the cross and answered, "I do indeed, Señorita."

"We were told," I continued, pleased by his reply, "that there is a ghost in this house."

"I know nothing of that, Señorita," he said, "but if such a thing were true, it would be a ghost of very high ranking."

I found his reply amusing. Father ignored the exchange and knocked on the front door. Just before he was about to knock again, a corpulent and most unghostlike woman, dressed as a maid, opened it.

"Good afternoon," Father said. "Might there be any member of the family in residence?"

"Who may I say is calling, sir?" the woman asked, drying her hands on her apron as she inspected Father, me, the cart, and its cargo with great suspicion.

"You may say that Shiro of Sendai is calling, and the grandniece of Doña Soledad Medina."

The woman, as round as she was tall, did not react to our names in any way. She only said, "Wait here please," before closing the door. I noticed she closed it gently.

I then realized how frivolous my humor and concerns were in that moment compared with Father's. For me, being on dry land in a new place, where the sun shone not too oppressively, was sufficient adventure. It was very different for him, and I suppose I knew it, and it made me nervous, so I preferred to talk about ghosts rather than pay attention to anything real from his past that might be connected to me.

Just as I was sobering to this thought, as the driver, zen as any monk in Kyoto, lit a pipe, as Father waited patiently at the door, and as I stood petting the mule's broad forehead, a young man slightly older than me appeared on horseback. He was handsome and dressed like a gentleman, and the horse, pure Arabian, was white and magnificent with its mane and tail braided to perfection. He dismounted

137

in one motion and looked at us with an expression of benevolent curiosity.

But before he could utter a single sound of greeting, the door to the house was opened again, this time by a different woman, a beautiful and elegant lady in her mid-thirties, wearing a long white dress offset by long, raven-black hair. It was Rosario. She and Father just stood there, staring at each other. The young man stared at them in turn—as did the driver and I. Then Rosario looked at me and began to weep.

– PART FIVE –

– XXIX –

I had little recollection of where I was taken to live in Venice as a child. The castle where I grew up in Japan was exquisite but austere. My brief impressions of Kurt's home in Amsterdam are confused with the romantic notions that began to flower there. I was not at all prepared for Rosario's home in Sanlúcar. Its combination of simplicity and sophistication, its whiteness with dark furnishings, the deeply waxed terracotta floor tiles, the Islamic arches, the placement of flowers and paintings, the sensation that no matter how much one was occupying an interior space, the exterior accompanied you as well.

Delicate vines of white jasmine crept through windows. Pots of thick green ferns lined upstairs hallways. A blue and yellow bird flew into the house from one of the gardens and fluttered about unperturbed. In the grand entrance hall, I saw my first portrait of the Duke of Medina-Sidonia, Father's patron, Rosario's late husband, and the young rider's sire. The solemnity and dignity of the painting and the richness of its gilded frame coexisted in unexpected harmony with the high, whitewashed walls surrounding it. The whitewash was chipped here and there, and spots of mold were visible near ceiling beams that were decorated with Moorish inlay. And all the while I felt the presence of the sea, the shore, the dunes, the estuary, and the Gulf of Cadiz. Clean light speckled on the palm trees, on the coverlets in the bedrooms, sluicing through the slats of dark green shutters.

The shock and emotion that gripped Rosario were such that her son Francisco and I soon left her alone with Father. Proud, shy, and well-mannered, the young man showed me about the house and grounds. Though surprised like his mother, he seemed much less affected by our sudden appearance and continuing existence in the world. We were, after all, just two characters from a story he had been told as a child, two ghosts suddenly become flesh. After inquiring politely about our journey—displaying, I should add, a remarkable lack of interest in what was an epic tale—he spent most of our time together that afternoon complaining about his provincial life, a constricted routine that was only relieved occasionally by visits to Sevilla, which, according to him, was not that much different.

Judging from his mother's reaction, I wondered how close she and Father had been during his convalescence in that house so many years before. She was recently widowed back then, and was carrying the self-involved young man walking beside me in her womb. She was alluring. From the first moment I felt drawn to her, yet I also felt somewhat jealous of her, a sensation that was new to me.

After the tour concluded, Francisco and I sat in the shade looking out at the garden near a quince tree that was heavy with fruit. He had run out of things to say, and though this made him anxious, I was content to sit in silence in continuing gratitude for being on terra firma. Then he noticed the satchel Father had placed by the travel trunk, where he had put our swords before mounting the cart in front of Dolores' house. The hilts were sticking out from it.

"What manner of sword are those your father carries?" Francisco asked.

"Samurai swords," I replied.

"And what, pray, are samurai?" he asked, adjusting his frilly cuffs in a manner that looked like a gesture he had learned to imitate.

"Samurai are Japanese nobles and warriors," I said. "And two of those swords are mine."

He seemed both shocked and intimidated, which pleased me. Then Father appeared and asked me to come with him back into the drawing room.

Rosario was sitting at the end of a large settee covered in thick burgundy velvet. She held a lace handkerchief, damp from tears, with both hands. Her beautiful dark eyes were still tinged with red. Otherwise, she seemed composed and appeared to be relieved, and she evinced an expression of hope and curiosity. The head of a bull, and two sets of antlers that had belonged to some species of mountain goat, hung on the wall behind her. A Persian carpet was on the floor in front of her, separating the settee from the two plush armchairs Father and I sat in. I remembered learning how the weavers of those carpets, so rich and complex in their design, always left a thread loose somewhere, so as not to commit a sin of pride, negating perfection, a state only permitted to Allah. I thought it was really a superstition that attempted to keep misfortune at bay.

"Rosario has told me many things," Father said, "some of them sad, some of them wondrous. But there is one thing that requires our setting out for Sevilla immediately."

"Surely you can spend the night," Rosario said. "Both of you must be exhausted. We might all of us leave at first light in our carriage."

Father considered it for a moment and then consented. "All right," he said. "That would be most kind."

Then he looked at me and continued. "Your Spanish grandfather, Don Rodrigo, and your half-brother died some years ago."

I looked at him, over to her, and then back at him again. In truth the news had little effect on me.

"Caitríona is alive and living in Sevilla," he said. "She gave birth to a son named Patrick, and then went on to marry your mother's brother Carlos, and has had a daughter with him."

"So I have a half-brother who is alive," I said.

"Yes."

"And you have a son."

"Yes," he replied, "a boy just four years younger than you."

I was not sure, in that moment, how I felt about this revelation. I suppose I feared the intrusion of a rival for the affection I had always taken for granted, and received exclusively, a rival in the form of a half-brother, the half-brother's mother, and then the woman sitting across from us.

"I thought my mother's brother was a priest," I said, in an attempt to ignore all of this news.

"He was," Rosario said, "or almost. But then he changed his mind."

I looked at her and did my best to smile. "Is there more?" I asked, assuming this to be the reason that, for some reason, necessitated the hurried journey to Sevilla.

"Yes," Father said.

I looked at him and prepared myself.

"Your Spanish grandmother, Inmaculada, is still alive and well, and so, it seems, is Doña Soledad Medina, your great-aunt."

I felt a little faint, without knowing why. I felt like crying, without knowing why.

"She is very old," Rosario said, speaking to me gently, "and bedridden, and she has not spoken to anyone for over two years."

"How old is she?" I asked.

"Close to ninety," she replied.

I looked down at the carpet, searching for the loose thread.

"She is still waiting for us," I said.

– XXX –

My first trip to Sevilla, in Rosario's elegant but termite ravaged carriage. The heat. Hills the color of lions. Stubborn, dark cork trees. Narrow streams. Pink and white oleanders lining the riverbeds. Francisco's furtive stares. The evening arrival at the city gates. The swallows racing through the sky as we crossed the Guadalquivir River—the river my mother and I had been baptized in.

We went straight to the Casa de Pilatos, and there I met my grandmother, Inmaculada, my other Mizuki, so different and yet similar in bearing. I saw parts of myself in her as we looked at each other, before she grasped me and cried. She embraced Father for the first time in her life. I met Caitríona again, who fainted immediately upon seeing us, and who might well have cracked her skull on the marble tiles had Father not rushed to catch her. She, too, was beautiful, with freckles and strong auburn hair. The emotions were intense. They ricocheted off the walls and the statues. It was almost too much for everyone.

When Caitríona revived and recovered, even as she was unable to take her eyes off Father and me, there was much discussion among the women as to how to prepare Doña Soledad for our appearance. My grandmother Inmaculada feared the shock might kill her. Caitríona worried she might not recognize us at all, being too far gone from the world, for too long a time. Father cut through the knot of feminine doubt, taking me by the wrist, and leading me directly up a grand flight of stairs, the adjacent walls covered with paintings. He brought me into the master bedroom suite.

A maid sat in an anteroom doing needlepoint. She was surprised and embarrassed by our sudden appearance, apologizing and

145

clumsily trying to hide her needles and threads. Father ignored her as I smiled at her. He almost dragged me into Doña Soledad's boudoir.

And there she was, illuminated by thick candles, propped up on wide pillows in a nightgown. Her hands, almost translucent, rested atop a crisp coverlet. She might have been dead. She resembled the cadaver of an old woman I once saw in Sendai. But then she blinked, and though it was labored and sometimes noisy, she breathed. Father, wisely and to my surprise, said nothing to her. He sat on the edge of the bed, up close to her and, reaching over her, patted a space on the other side of her, indicating where I should sit.

At first her gaze did not alter, for her watery eyes were open, directed at the ceiling. I looked up and saw a series of dark beams inlaid with bits of ivory that formed an intricate design, an Islamic text of some sort. We sat there for a minute or two, while my grand-mother Inmaculada and Caitríona and Rosario entered the room, hovering back by the doorway. Father was patient. It was as if he knew what would happen, while the rest of us, including the maid who crept up behind the other ladies, waited in dubious anticipation.

And then, all of a sudden, her eyes went from staring at the ceiling to staring at Father's face. I could see she was examining him. Then she took his hand, and in a very small voice, she asked him, "Am I dreaming?"

I could feel the astonishment and the emotions of the women in the doorway at hearing her speak, and it flowed into me as well.

"No, Señora," father said. "We are here, with you."

Then she looked at me and gasped, a gasp that stirred her entire fragile being, and she began to cry. She tried to lean forward. She released Father's hand and grabbed both of mine in both of hers. Her grip was strong.

"Is it you, dear?" she asked. "*Solete?*"

"Yes, Aunt," I replied, crying now myself. "It is I."

Father helped her to lean forward. She was light, like a bird. She could not take her eyes from me, nor was I able to avert my gaze from her. Letting go of one of my hands, she felt my hair that barely reached my shoulders. She felt my forehead, my cheeks and neck. She felt my breasts. Father moved her toward me, and I took hold of her, almost as if she were a child. She was sobbing, and so were the others. I held her and rocked her the smallest amount, terrified I might break a fragile bone.

"You're alive," she said through her tears. "You've come home."

Father retreated, and the women of the house gathered round the bed and joined in the conversation, demonstrating a solidarity that, with the exception of some tensions here and there over the following months, managed to endure. The maid brought everyone bowls of a clear, hot soup, and we stayed with my great-aunt until she fell asleep. The other women encouraged me to lay my head next to hers for the night, and they brought in my nightgown and another coverlet. I blew out all of the candles save for one and lay there in the darkness, listening to this woman who was so close to me and yet such a stranger. Eventually I too succumbed to slumber.

I woke in the middle of the night and realized again how selfish I had been. Father knew this woman well, had lived with her and my mother during some of the happiest months of his life. It had cost him a great deal to leave her and then cost him more—much more than I have attempted to describe—to return. She, like I— more than I in a way—was living proof of a past that was important to him. Nevertheless, he had devoted all his charm and energy that evening toward handing me back to her. I had not thought about, or asked, how he might be feeling. And he had still to meet his son.

As these thoughts wound their way through me, my aunt turned and found me there. She looked better in the dim light.

"How good of you to have stayed here with me," she said in a stronger version of the Sevillano accent I had learned.

"Father didn't want you to wake and worry that perhaps you had made it all up."

"And you?"

"I'm fine. It's lovely here."

"When last we saw each other, you were barely two. You could barely talk. Now you're a beautiful young woman. I thought I'd never see you again."

"Many things got in the way."

"But you are all right."

"Oh yes."

"And you are Japanese now."

"Yes."

"But you smell like your mother."

"I do? Is it a good smell?"

"My dear, it is the best scent in this world."

"What is it like?" I asked, rolling over onto my stomach to get a better look at her. I felt like a child again.

"It is a mixture of things," she said, thinking about it. "Orange blossom. Boxwood. A touch of grapefruit rind. Wet dogs."

"Wet dogs?"

"Few things smell better than a dog come in from the rain, after it shakes itself."

I giggled when she said this, and the noise of my giggle pleased her.

"You were there when I was born, no, Aunt? When Mother died."

"It was the saddest day of my life," she said, "and one of the reasons I love you so."

Carefully, I squeezed her hand.

"How can you love me," I said, "if you do not know me?"

"Are you a wicked girl?"

"Sometimes."

"Do you love your father?"

"Very much."

"Then that, and who your mother was, is all I need to know. Will you let me take care of you, for the little time I have left?"

"You mustn't leave me now," I said. "Now that I've finally arrived."

"I shall do my best."

Her room was so big, the house was so big, and the enclosed garden below so vast, it was hard to believe we were surrounded by a city.

"Tell me," she said, "what did they call you in Japan?"

"Masako."

"Masako," she said, repeating it just as I had pronounced it. "Does it mean anything?"

"It means something like . . . a proper child."

"There. You see? You cannot be wicked with a name like that. Is that what I should call you?"

"My first name was Soledad María. Father always said I was named after you."

"That you were. Do you know what it means, Soledad?"

"Lonely, or loneliness."

"Sí. Perhaps it's too sad a name for you."

"I've been Masako for as long as I can remember."

"So that is what we shall call you."

I thought about it. I thought about what all of this might mean to her.

"You can call me however you wish," I said.

"Then I shall call you Solete," she said. "Which could also mean something like a small sun, a little star in the heavens."

– XXXI –

Members of the Fugger family—my great-aunt's German bankers—and a notary were summoned the following morning. They were shown directly to her bedroom. I could see by their body language, nervous tics, coat and belt adjustments, beard preening and such, that they were both pleased and intimidated to be there. What probably began as an ordinary, sedentary day for them had been transformed into an event they would impress colleagues with for a long time afterward.

Documents relating to my inheritance were retrieved, presented, reviewed, and re-ratified in the presence of witnesses who read and signed them. My grandmother Inmaculada and Rosario hovered about like guardian angels. The ceremony made me uncomfortable, but my aunt told me, as we were waiting for the three rotund men, that she wished for people to see her in her right mind certifying what she had put into writing when I was two. "The only sin in Sevilla more prevalent than envy is avarice," she said. "Once I am gone, I will not be able to protect you, so I wish to make my intentions clear to everyone yet again."

Seeing as how I had reached the age of adulthood, Father was no longer included as a beneficiary. But I left everything in his hands. He was the only person in the world I trusted. He was not present that morning. He had more urgent business, meeting his son for the first time—my half-brother Patrick. Uncle Carlos was away in Granada, as he often was back then, hunting and spending time with his comrade Hermenegildo, and Hermenegildo's strident wife, Ana María Angustias.

Caitríona and my brother later told me how the meeting went. Patrick was fifteen years old then, handsome but timid, and he spent most of that first encounter staring at the floor. His eyes were Asian like mine, and there was a slight ochre tone to his smooth skin. Like his mother, he had freckles on his nose and cheeks. He was strong and tall. Reared as a Spanish gentleman, he was understandably confused by Father's presence. All during his childhood Caitríona had told her son many things about Father's exploits, the men he had killed, the friends he had made in high places—kings and dukes, the shogun and the pope—and she had emphasized how much of the Earth he had seen on his travels.

My Uncle Carlos had done all he could to make his stepson embarrassed about his Asian heritage, to consider it a blemish he should endeavor to hide. His Spanish cousins and schoolmates made fun of him, and many elders spoke to him derisively. But there, all of a sudden on that morning, was the man he had always assumed to be dead, the samurai warrior wearing strange clothes and swords, with jet-black hair pulled back into a tight tail that curved upward. His father was a foreigner like no other, and un-Christian, the bastard who had made him a bastard as well.

"I am so pleased to meet you," Father said, rather stiffly, with a curt bow, very like him, though his eyes were moist with emotion.

"And I you, sir," my brother replied.

"You've grown into an impressive young man," Father said, patting my brother three times on the shoulder. The gesture made Patrick even more uncomfortable, and Father saw it, and retreated back into his shell. An awkward silence ensued. Father and son looked to Caitríona for assistance.

"It will take time," she said to them, "for you to come to know each other."

Father made a brief noise of assent the way Japanese men do.

"He has grown up here in Sevilla," Caitríona continued. "He has grown up believing, like me, that you were no longer in this world."

"I am not so easy to kill," Father said.

Part of that was bragging, part of it a simple fact. Caitríona blushed and looked away.

"And I am a Christian, sir," my brother then said.

Father looked back at him.

"Are you now?" he said. "That is logical. Living here among them, that is sensible. But now that I am back, I will teach you how to speak Japanese, and educate you about the other side of your soul."

"I do not think I will be allowed to do that," my brother said.

"Who," Father asked, "would prevent you from learning something so interesting?"

"My father," Patrick said. It just slipped out. Immediately, he realized how strange a thing it was to have uttered.

"I am your father," Father said.

"Yes," my brother replied. "I know. I am sorry. I meant Don Carlos."

"Don Carlos and I shall speak about this."

Once again, they both looked to Caitríona. But this time, mesmerized from watching the two of them together, face to face, she was the one at a loss for words.

"Where was he born?" Father asked her gently.

"In Sicily," Caitríona replied.

Then Father turned to my brother.

"Your mother and I have much to talk about," he said, bowing again.

My brother did not bow back. He did not know what to do. He was eager to end the conversation. But then he thought of something.

"Is it true," he asked, "that you have slain many men with your sword?"

Father looked at him for a few seconds before responding. Father later said it was then that he saw in the boy his own flesh and blood, and it overwhelmed him.

"I have done what I had to," Father replied. "Would you like to learn how to use this sword? I have already taught your sister."

Father drew his katana and showed it to the boy. Then he took a handkerchief from his kimono and tossed it up in the air. He used the sword to cut it into three pieces. My brother caught one of the strips as it floated to the ground.

Caitríona and Father's attentions were focused on their son that day. Some time would pass before I was able to ask her how it felt to be standing next to him again. Did they recall, during any of the moments they stood there with the bashful adolescent dressed like a Sevillano dandy, when and where they had made him? Father later told me how beautiful he found her, that she was even more beautiful than he remembered, that the intervening years had transformed her girlish air and granted her an even more compelling allure.

After the business of my inheritance was concluded, and Doña Soledad went back to sleep, I went with my grandmother to Caitríona's house to meet Patrick myself. Rosario and Francisco remained at the Casa de Pilatos. My brother found conversation with me easier. He was close to my grandmother, and this too helped. It also allowed Father and Caitríona to speak together in private. It was then that they were able to tell each other all that had happened to them since their separation. She wept when she told him about her decision to marry Carlos. Father listened calmly as she described the situation, the arrangement they had, and how Carlos had become more conservative and severe since his father's death, since becoming a grandee of Spain, since being accepted and esteemed at court in Madrid. She said he still wanted her to produce a male heir for him, but that she did not wish to be with him in that way ever again. She told Father about Hermenegildo, how the noble-man from Granada had married a woman who also put up with her husband's nature.

Then she had the governess fetch her daughter, Carlota, who was eight years old, a gaunt little girl with chestnut hair. Father lifted her up and made jokes with her, and this too made Caitríona weep. I watched them from the corner of my eye and saw what a handsome couple they made, and I struggled to remember when the three of us had been together in Venice, in Greece, in Egypt, and in India. I wondered what might happen. It was clear that Father and Rosario also had strong feelings for each other. After so many years of living without any romance in his life, of having to resort to women in brothels, he was now confronted with two very beautiful and engag-ing ladies whom he had been strongly attached to, in relationships that had been interrupted rather than ended.

All of us took the midday meal together in the Casa de Pilatos: Father and I, Caitríona and Patrick and little Carlota, Rosario and Francisco, and my grandmother Inmaculada, who sat where Doña Soledad would have. Conversation was strained at first, until Francisco asked Father what the Duke of Medina-Sidonia had been like.

"Surely your mother has told you about him," Father replied.

"She has told me what she wished to. But I would like to hear about him from you, who were so close to him," Francisco said, looking very handsome that day. I could see that Patrick looked up to him. I hoped that the fact that Francisco in turn looked up to Father might prove helpful in opening my brother's heart some more. Father may have sensed it too, for he went on to regale us all with amusing and moving anecdotes regarding the duke. I suspect it was also a way for him to begin feeling his way back into the reality of Spain.

After finishing the meal with some fruit, the group went off to the garden to sip infusions of herbs. I stayed behind with my grandmother Inmaculada. It was the first time we were alone together.

"Seeing you here before me," she said, "it is as if you have descended from heaven. I never saw you after you were born."

"Why was that?" I asked her. I hoped she could tell from my tone that it was not an accusation.

"We disapproved," she said, and then hesitated. "I was going to say my husband especially, but that is not true. Both of us were ashamed of your mother, and ashamed of you. She already had a child, a son and heir, with the man she had married."

"The husband who impregnated her by force," I said. "The one who cut off my father's finger and broke my father's hands. The one she never loved."

These words did come out of me as an accusation. But I said it quietly, as a simple statement of fact.

"The one your father killed," she agreed in a tone similar to mine. "She did love Julian, at first. That was his name. She loved him at the very beginning, when she was very young and eager to marry him."

"Nevertheless," I said, choosing to ignore this, "I'm glad he's dead."

She looked down.

"As am I," she said.

"You were ashamed because your daughter fell in love with a Japanese man, and had a child out of wedlock."

"It was a terrible scandal," she said. "You must try and imagine it. I do not know how these things are tolerated in Japan, but here they are considered mortal sins. Neither my husband nor I were brought up to condone such a thing."

"And yet your aunt did condone it, or accepted it," I said, "the woman I am named for, a woman very high on your social scale."

155

"Yes," she said. "And I regret what I did. This is what I wish for you to know. I regret it. I didn't at first. I held on to my spite and to my prejudices for a time, for far too long a time. To tell you the absolute truth, I did not recognize how terrible my sin was, until my husband and grandson died, and I was left alone in the world. It was only then that I missed my daughter. It was only then that I realized how terrible I had been to her, how I had wished for her to be as unhappy in her marriage as I had been in mine. I realized how jealous and contemptuous of her I had been at seeing her so happy with your father. When she died after giving birth to you, I convinced myself it was because God wished to punish her. Over time I came to hate myself for it."

A silence ensued, and then she said something else.

"You look like her."

"Who?" I said, knowing full well who she meant.

"Your mother."

"I also look like my father," I said.

"You are very beautiful," she said. "You must know that."

"I am a half-breed," I said, "and a bastard."

"You are my granddaughter," she said, trying her best to win me. "You are my flesh and blood. You are all I have left of the daughter I brought into this world, and then treated so selfishly before losing her. And now you are here. I can reach out and touch you. I wish for us to get along. I do not want to lose you. I want to try and treat you the way I should have treated her."

I took her hand. It seemed a natural thing to do. It surprised her. I could see she was not accustomed to being touched.

"Then again," I said, "if you had treated her better, perhaps she would have married someone else, perhaps she would never have met or fallen in love with my father. So, in a way, I have you to thank for my existence."

156

Making an effort, and I could tell it was an effort, she covered our two hands with her other hand.

"What an odd way to look at life," she said. But she uttered it merely to say something. What most occupied her attention at that moment, I think, was the sensation of having my hand between hers.

"I have not descended from the heavens," I said. "I have come on a most extraordinary journey, back from Japan where I left another grandmother behind."

"I know," she said. "It is a miracle I thank God for. I celebrate it."

"I have already been disappointed by one grandmother," I said. "I would like for us to do better."

"We shall, dear," she said. "I will see to it. What happened with your father's mother in Japan?"

I told her the story of where and how we lived. I placed emphasis on the splendor of Date Masamune's castle, so that she would not think me intimidated by my newfound wealth in Sevilla. I described the evolution of my relationship with Mizuki, how much she had meant to me when I was little, how secure and loved she made me feel, how well she had educated me in the manners of the emperor's court, and then, as I grew older, how she changed, culminating with the horrible tale of how she had been implicated in the cruel demise of Yokiko. Doña Inmaculada listened carefully, patiently, and then said the following.

"Perhaps you've got it wrong, Soledad," she said—for she would never call me by my Japanese name. "It sounds to me like your Japanese grandmother saved your life, and quite intentionally."

"How do you mean?" I asked.

"If she had not poisoned this other woman," she said, "your father would not have left. She knew it would ruin her bond with the person she most cared for in this world: your father. She knew it would result in his taking you away from her. It freed you, and freed your father. It provided the impetus for him to bring you back here in time, before your life there would have changed irrevocably. I think she did what she did because of her love for you, and that it must have been an enormous sacrifice."

I had never considered what happened in this light. Neither had Father. I began to weep at the thought it might be true. Mizuki had, in pure Buddhist fashion, let go of her most beloved attachments, liberating me and Father both before entering the nunnery, her life all but over. She, who had been the great beauty of Sendai. I was seized with a necessity to tell her that I understood, to tell her how well the stratagem had worked, to tell her that we had survived the journey. I needed to tell her how sorry I was for not seeing it, until my mother's mother saw it for me. Even though I could never forgive her for Yokiko's death, I needed to tell her how grateful I was to her for having taken such good care of me. I resolved to write it down in a letter and to beg Kurt Vanderhooven, when next I saw him, to try and see that it might reach her before she died.

– XXXII –

Doña Soledad was eager for me to visit my mother's grave. Father was not prepared to return there yet, but he encouraged me to go if I wished. He told me it would make him feel good to know I had reached the place where I was born, an estate that would one day be mine. When Caitríona offered to accompany me, he seemed to waver in his resolve. But in the end, seeing as how she was still married—to my uncle no less—he returned to Sanlúcar with Rosario and Francisco. Doña Inmaculada remained with Doña Soledad in Sevilla. As a gesture to please my great-aunt, I changed into one of the finer dresses I had acquired in Amsterdam. It was made from thick silk dyed the color of eggplant. When I came into Doña Soledad's bedroom to say goodbye, my grandmother Inmaculada put her hand to her mouth in shock and said, "How beautiful you look. For a moment I thought you were Guada."

Doña Soledad held out her hand for me to take.

"Very beautiful indeed," she said. "But there's no need for you to dress this way for me."

"I thought it might please you," I said.

"It is you that pleases me," she said, "no matter what you choose to wear or call yourself."

I could see the comment irked my grandmother somewhat, and I suspected Doña Soledad had made a point of saying it in her presence. I kissed her hand.

"Thank you," I said. And then I bowed to her and said it again in Japanese, "*Arigato*."

She insisted that Caitríona and I take her finest carriage. It was large and painted sky blue with gold trimmings. Inside the seats were covered in navy velvet and the rounded ceiling was adorned with cherubs, depicting the Virgin Mary's ascension into heaven. Four spirited horses pulled it, and a footman in livery rode at the back. The driver, Narciso, well on in years, had been in Doña Soledad's service since his childhood. He wore thick corduroy breeches and a brown greatcoat.

The journey was beautiful and relatively smooth. Rains had replenished the rivers and brooks. Wet leaves littered the roadsides, and some of the trees were bare. But there were vast expanses of olive groves, and the grass covering fallow farmland was a vibrant green. On the first part of the trip, Caitríona and I sat next to each other with Carlota between us. My brother Patrick sat opposite, next to Carlota's governess. He pretended to study the scenery but kept stealing glances at me whenever he thought me distracted. His presence inhibited his mother and me from broaching topics we were eager to discuss. He was glum and still confused, no doubt, by our intrusion into his world. His unhappiness expressed itself through complaints about having nothing to do at La Moratalla.

"Nonsense," Caitríona said, peeved and disappointed at his refusal to show me a better side of his nature. "You've been there countless times, and always enjoy it."

"That is not true," he said. But he looked down as he said it, embarrassed, knowing that he was lying.

"Why are you being so difficult?" Caitríona asked him, plainly frustrated. "What is your sister to make of you?

"My half-sister," he said in an odious tone, pretending to gaze out the window.

After we stopped for a light meal that we had brought with us, I left them to argue below as I, to their surprise, opted to sit up top with the driver. He was disconcerted at first, but after a while I was able to put him at ease. I asked him if he had known my mother.

"I did, madam," he said. "It was this carriage that brought her, Doña Soledad, a priest, and your grandparents to the river's edge in Sevilla for her baptism. No one in the nobility had ever done such a thing. Babies were always baptized in the cathedral. The priest was arguing against it the whole time, but Doña Soledad and your grandfather ignored him. Then your mother traveled with me a number of times in her youth, and sat up here with me like you, once or twice. And I brought her along this very same route, from Sevilla to La Moratalla, on her wedding day."

All of this made a strong impression on me.

"She spent her wedding night at La Moratalla?" I asked.

"Yes, madam," he said. "And I brought her here as well when she was carrying you. When she came here with her little boy and with your father and Doña Soledad." He gave out this latter bit of intelligence quickly, as if to deflect my attention from the one before it.

"What were people's opinions about my father back then," I said, "and about me?"

"That is not for me to say, madam."

"What did *you* think then?"

"I never liked Don Julian," he said matter-of-factly. "Not many people did. With your father I never exchanged a word. But he always impressed me as a genuine *caballero*, a real gentleman, even though—"

He realized he was on the verge of saying something that might offend me, and did not finish his thought.

"Even though he was a heathen," I said, smiling at him.

He saw the smile and was grateful for it.

"*Eso*," he said. "I cannot speak for the wealthy and noble families, but people like me respected him for how he behaved."

161

"And how about me," I asked him, "a heathen girl born out of wedlock?"

"Doña Soledad has made you her heir," he said. "Everyone knows this. It will influence everyone's opinions, except for the priests. As for whether one's parents are married or not, it seems a small thing to me. And people always enjoy scandal, no matter what is said in public."

"You are a wise man, Narciso," I said.

I could hear mother and son arguing below, and I thought about how odd life was, considering how Caitríona and my father had met, how my own existence had brought them together, how much in love they had once been on the island of Paxos where the boy, my half-brother, had been conceived, all of the trauma everyone had gone through afterward. And now the boy was grown and speaking to her with bitterness as we approached the Andalusian estate where Father had also been so in love with my mother.

"How old is this carriage, Narciso?" I asked.

"I am not good with numbers," he replied. "It was a wedding gift to Doña Soledad from her parents. It brought her to the cathedral on the day she was married. It brought her to the funerals of her husband, and then her two sons. My father was the driver then. He drove for her until he was too old, and that is when I took over."

That evening after supper, as my brother sulked off to bed and Caitríona spoke in the kitchen with the staff about our meals and our stay there, I walked through the massive drawing rooms, amazed at the fact that they would someday be mine. I thought about the carriage. It was outside at that hour in the dark. The horses were in the stables. Narciso and the other gentleman had disappeared into some part of the enormous house as yet unknown to me. The carriage had brought my great-aunt to her wedding, ferried my mother to her baptism, transported Mother and Father from Sevilla to La

Moratalla when I was in her womb, when all they expected from life was happiness. When not in use, it spent most of its time parked in a long cobblestone entryway adjacent to the Casa de Pilatos, as the city swirled about it. With its beautifully shaped doors and golden hinges, its plush seats and tall spoked wheels, it had been there during my entire life, my mother's life, and almost all of Doña Soledad's life. The persistence of things, of inanimate objects, obsessed me.

Standing there in that house where my mother and her great-aunt had grown up deep in the Andalusian countryside, I knew that at the very same moment, on the other side of the world, my bedroom in the Sendai Castle existed as well: its sliding doors that smelled of cedar, the floor mats, the sound of the fountain and the crickets from the garden just outside, were just as real as the ones I could hear then. The abandoned river skiffs in North America that we discovered by the gravesite of Fernando de Alarcón were just where we left them, there on that immense and wild continent where Father taught me to survive. The remains of Lonan's body were as real and existent as the carriage parked outside. Kurt was somewhere in the West Indies. People with their fragile bodies, filled with blood, bones, organs, and fleeting emotions, skittered about from birth to death, surrounded by things and places that stayed put, indifferent. Mizuki was in a monastery somewhere near Kyoto. Doña Inmaculada was at the bedside of Doña Soledad. Mother was buried nearby on the estate somewhere.

***

I was relieved when Caitríona joined me, distracting me from my maudlin meditations. It was good to be with someone alive and youthful. We sat on armchairs in the library, facing a balcony that overlooked the large central fountain that was bathed in moonlight.

I expected her to speak of my brother, to try to explain his behavior, or to ask me what it felt like to be in Spain. But Caitríona was Caitríona. She didn't say anything at first, and when she did, she spoke in English with that Irish lilt in her voice. She took my hand and held it as we sat there, as Inmaculada had done, but in this case the gesture was infinitely more natural.

"I wonder if my mother is still alive," she said.

All I could do was squeeze her hand.

"Sometimes I wish her dead, and hope it happened quickly," she said.

Both of us knew that was unlikely.

"We could try to find her," I said. "Perhaps Father could attempt it, with gold to offer."

"No," she said. "If she's not dead she will have adjusted by now, and she would die from the shame of it. Your father has done enough rescuing you and me and all the rest of it. He deserves some peace now."

"He needs to be with someone too," I said. "It has been a long time for him without real female companionship. You are fortunate to be married."

She looked at me, incredulous. "Is it possible you do not know about your uncle Carlos?"

"In what regard?" I asked.

"He does not fancy women," she said. "He fancies men. Our marriage is one of convenience. He desired respectability and a child. I wanted security for Patrick and me."

"I had no idea," I said. "Father never spoke of it, and he is not prudish about such things. You should leave him if you are unhappy. I will take care of you, and my brother, and Carlota. It would give me great joy to do so."

"What might your future husband say about that?" she asked with a smile.

164

"It shall be none of his business," I replied. "I would never marry anyone who might try to dissuade me against it. I have not escaped being the consort of a monster in Japan and crossed the world to end up the wife of an intruder."

I told myself I meant it. I was trying on this new me, a woman who would have independent means, perhaps one of the few in the world.

"Why should you do that for me?" she asked.

"Because you took care of me, Caitríona. Because you are the mother of my brother. Because I would have been lost and annihilated without you."

"The truth is that you took care of me," she said. "You would have been fine without me. The pirate beast would never have harmed you. You were too valuable to him. And his poor mistress adored you. I often wonder about Maria Elena. She was not a bad person. It was you who saved my life."

"Be that as it may," I said, "from the moment they took Father off that ship until that horrible day when we were separated at sea, I was in your care, for thousands of hours and kilometers."

We finished our wine, opened the balcony doors, and stepped outside. It was cold and quiet, except for the noise of the fountain. The lemon trees were bare, the plane trees denuded, the quince trees mottled with swollen fruit. It smelled of boxwood and damp and smoke from fires that were lit in the hearths throughout the house.

"I think I am going to like it here," I said.

"Yes," she said. "You will."

"You must stay with us here always," I said.

She put her arm around me and drew me in.

"We shall see," she said.

On the following morning I made a point of wearing a kimono. Caitríona took me through the formal gardens and up into the

165

unkempt wood where the grave was. It was set back in a clearing by two columns, remnants of what had been a small Roman temple. The grass was long and moist and very green. I read my mother's name on her tombstone where a Biwa tree grew. A few meters behind it, the clearing came to an end, up against a wall of shrubbery. Caitríona walked with me there. Through a gap, she pointed out the Guadalquivir River down below, snaking peacefully between the green rolling fields that spread out in the distance, south and west toward the town of Palma del Río. Where the fields blended into a morning haze in the distance, the dark northern side of the Sierra Morena Mountains rose up. She remained there while I returned to the grave. I stared at it for some time and tried to feel something. I was sad, of course, but more than sadness, I felt wonder. For the first time since our arrival, I felt like I was home.

– XXXIII –

We spent the rest of the morning strolling around the gardens with Carlota and her governess. The little girl insisted I tell her what everything we passed was called in Japanese. Caitríona introduced me to the rest of the staff and to the gardeners. After the midday meal when Patrick wished to go for a ride and his mother disapproved, I offered to accompany him. He did not expect this, but he was pleased to have his way. I put on a pair of *umanori hakama,* samurai trousers that were ideal for riding. Caitríona, the stable hands, and Patrick were shocked to see me reject one of Doña Soledad's sidesaddles. I took my horse by the mane and swung up astride it. I told them that Japanese saddles were just as ornate and cumbersome as the Spanish variety—for I did not wish for them to think I came from a primitive culture—but that for many months during the previous year I had ridden virtually bareback. Caitríona was most amused.

I allowed Patrick to lead the way, and after cantering and galloping and giving me what I assumed was his best impression of how his stepfather wished him to comport himself, he finally relaxed when we rested the horses at the river. I told him about our journey from Japan and of our adventures in Santa Fe on the new continent, our battles, our escapes, the soldiers we had to kill, our interactions with the various tribes of natives. I told him I had fallen in love with a Zuni brave who died in battle. He followed the tale, enraptured, and asked many questions. He wondered, as I often had, what had become of the horses we let free before paddling over to New Amsterdam. Sometimes when he spoke, I saw Father in him, and myself, in ways that gave me shivers. It occurred to me that part of my task in Spain was to learn and adapt to its ways, and that for Patrick the opposite was now true. By the time we returned to the house we'd become friends.

"Now you've two half-sisters," I said to him, as we walked the horses to the stables.

He smiled, then asked if I could teach him how to use a Japanese sword.

"You must ask Father for that," I said. "He is far more patient than I."

That evening, I ached from the ride, though I confessed it to no one. After supper we sat in front of burning olive logs by one of the tall hearths that were framed in green Italian marble. Sometimes small jets of blue flame would escape from inside the logs. Carlota fell asleep in my arms and Patrick, his guard down, sat on the rug nearby, drawing pictures of bloody battles. Soon, he too fell asleep, for we had allowed him wine at supper. Caitríona and I spoke of men. I told her about Lonan and Kurt. She, for obvious reasons, was far more discreet, although her description of how Carlota was conceived made us both laugh so hard the little girl woke up. I felt comfortable and happy in her presence, with none of the instinctual jealousy that seized me when I met Rosario.

I tried to remember how she and Father looked on Paxos when I was little, when I saw them naked on top of each other and swimming together. And then I reflected on how they looked standing side by side in Sevilla, and I liked it. I felt guilty and sorry for Rosario, who, all in all, had lived a lonelier life in Sanlúcar than Caitríona did at La Moratalla, Carmona, and Sevilla. Caitríona had borne Father a son and me a brother. She was younger and foreign like me, and had fire in her. That night, her story with Father seemed too romantic not to end with their being together again. We slept in the same bed, and fell asleep talking in the dark, as I'm told sisters often do.

A messenger arrived the next day from the Casa de Pilatos. He brought a letter from my grandmother summoning us back to Sevilla forthwith.

– XXXIV –

"Even when I was young, I often wondered when this day would arrive."

Doña Soledad said it in a whisper. Her skin was waxen and thin as gauze, her hair reduced to random strands of white that Doña Inmaculada had arranged in a dignified manner. I sat on the bed close to her, like I had that first day. My grandmother sat on the other side. The archbishop of Sevilla had just performed the Christian rite of Extreme Unction, and a spot of scented oil glistened on my great-aunt's forehead. The towering, venerated cleric smelled of garlic, and stood murmuring prayers on the fringes of the room, beside Caitríona and my Uncle Carlos, who had just arrived. My uncle was handsome and arrayed in a great luxury of fur and silk and velvet. He greeted me with gravity, with nary a smile. It was hard to judge whether the lack of sympathy in that first salutation was owing to the somber occasion at hand, or to his idea of me in general. I did not care. I was too occupied with giving thanks that Father and I had reached Sevilla after our journey, in time for Doña Soledad to see me alive and well.

Almost an hour passed before she spoke again, two phrases that were impossible to interpret. One was, "Be careful in the pasture." The other was, "Mind the stream, it's deep there." Her last words however, rang clear and shocked everyone, except for Caitríona and me. "Take off my clothes and ravish me," she commanded, weakly, but with yearning. Then spittle emerged from her lips and she choked on it. The choking became a cough that rattled her emaciated body. I imagine the strain of it stopped her heart. Once she was still, my grandmother wiped her mouth clean and gently shut her eyes. The archbishop came forward again, somewhat to my irritation, bending over her, and making the sign of the cross with cloying theatricality.

Father and Rosario and Francisco arrived in time for the funeral. She was laid to rest within a grand pantheon, joining her parents and her sons. Sevilla's elite attended the holy mass and the procession. Rather than being a day of mourning for them, it had the air of a social event. Apart from a modicum of seriousness the nobility maintained within the church during the ceremony, friends and distant relatives, dressed in their finery, used the occasion to speak animatedly with each other. Women used their fans as accoutrements, even though the day was overcast and brisk. It was so very different from burial rites in Japan, and those of the Zuni. Ironically, tellingly, my Uncle Carlos and Doña Inmaculada were the center of everyone's attention. Hermenegildo and his wife, who had accompanied my uncle from Granada, were there as well.

Without asking my permission or consulting me in any way, everyone repaired to the Casa de Pilatos after the burial. My grandmother, in her restrained manner, treated me with affection and respect throughout, but made only minimal efforts to introduce me as her grandchild. Uncle Carlos did nothing to hide what I can only describe as his disdain and displeasure at my presence.

Caitríona had warned me on the carriage ride from La Moratalla back to Sevilla. "He grew accustomed, as we all did, to the idea that you and your father were dead. It was easier for me to bear in my heart, and it was convenient for him. The only one that held out any hope at all was Doña Soledad. I know for a fact that once she died, he was going to try and use his newfound influence to claim your inheritance for himself."

"But he is well provided for, I assume," I said.

"Quite," she replied. "We, or I should say he, has more property and wealth than he knows what to do with. But what he most cares about in this world are the properties you are inheriting. They are the finest and grandest there are."

Patrick followed our conversation and, obviously conflicted, said not a word.

The tension that started to gather on the morning of the funeral erupted in full force once all the guests departed the house. Seeing little point in bidding farewell to people who had not paid me any attention, except to gawk, Father, Rosario, Caitríona, little Carlota, and I retired to a tranquil corner of the large enclosed garden. Patrick had gone off somewhere with Francisco.

Uncle Carlos emerged from the house and approached us. As he did, I noticed Hermenegildo and his wife loitering, like buzzards, in the background. I watched Doña Inmaculada retreating back into the house, away from her son. Her gait, and the way she was leaning forward, seemed to express displeasure. She had probably been urging her firstborn to calm himself, to reconsider, to be realistic, or to at least wait for a more civilized moment, and she had failed. He addressed Father first.

"I would like to speak with you alone," he said.

"If you are going to say something unpleasant," Father replied, "my daughter should hear it as well."

They stared at each other. Having met for the first time that morning, each one's existence still provoked the other. I think Father searched for traces of my mother in my uncle's face. Uncle Carlos sized up the man who had become a family legend, the man his sister had loved and died for, the man his parents had vilified, the man his wife had lost her virginity to and borne a child for, a much too foreign man, a heathen who dressed oddly. Then he looked at Caitríona.

"Would you and Rosario excuse us, please?"

Caitríona took Carlota by the hand, but gave her over to Rosario. "Would you mind?" she said. "I'd like to stay here for this."

Rosario, who my uncle also disapproved of due to her humble birth, smiled and replied, "Not at all," before walking off with the little girl.

Carlos looked at his spouse with a scowl. Then he turned to me.

"I recognize you are my niece," he said, as if he were the king himself, "my beloved sister's daughter. I recognize that our dearly departed aunt has favored you with the inheritance of her estate, a decision bordering on the insane. I will not contest it—with one exception. I cannot permit you to own and live in this house."

For the first time in a long while—out of the corner of my eye—I saw Father place both hands on the hilt of his long sword. I remained calm.

"Why is that?" I asked my uncle.

"I am a grandee of Spain," he said. "My family—"

"Our family," I said, interrupting him.

"My family," he insisted, "has been an eminent one in Sevilla since the reconquest. They built this house. This house is regarded as a palace in this city, where, it has always been assumed, that only someone of the highest station would reside."

I should note here—for it is one of the things I was grateful to Father for—that in the normal course of events, someone of my age and gender would not have been permitted to carry on this sort of conversation with someone like my uncle. In the normal course of events, my father would have ignored me, and answered for me. He—mostly—did no such thing.

"How much would you pay for it?" I asked my uncle.

This caught him by surprise.

"Pay for it," he repeated.

"Yes," I said. "If you want it so badly and since legally the property is mine, I assume you would wish to purchase it. Or perhaps we could arrange an exchange, your parents' house and the one given to you and Caitríona by Doña Soledad as a wedding gift. Together they must add up to approximately the ground covered by this one."

"Are you mad?" he said, quite aggressively.

"That's enough," Father said, quietly, but in a manner no one would wish to question. My uncle looked at him and his face paled.

"Uncle," I said. "You have insulted me in myriad ways, with great economy I might add, and on this day of all days, a day of mourning. I am astonished."

I had thought, since Caitríona had seen fit to marry him, since he was the only brother of the woman Father had loved so dearly, that there would be a tender side to his nature. Clearly, he had suffered greatly at the hands of his own family, and it had filled him with bile.

"Where does such greed and anger come from?" I asked him. "What wound, what grudge, has put you into such a frenzy of disrespect for your only niece?"

"Your presence here is an embarrassment to me," he replied, further fouling the air between us. "You are a glaring reminder of my sister's sinful folly. Your father's presence here threatens the reputation of my wife and stepson. I am sure tongues are already singing with scandal. For you to live in this house, in this city, is simply too much. I shall do all I must to wrest it from you."

Father was livid. I could feel it. My uncle turned to leave.

"Come, Caitríona," he said.

"No," she replied.

"Come, I say."

"No," she said again.

He stared at her, dumbfounded. Having managed to adroitly sever ties with the people who might have been of comfort to him, I almost felt sorry for him.

"From this moment forward," Caitríona said, "I shall be your wife in name only."

"You shall be my wife in whatever way I see fit," he said. "Like it or not."

"No," she said. "I shan't. I fulfilled my end of our bargain, Carlos. I married you in front of your provincial world. I even gave you a child. But that is all I shall do. I will not make a fuss, but my son and I, and our daughter, will live with you no longer, and if you wish to have a male heir of your own so badly, take a mistress."

"It's him, isn't it?" my uncle said, pointing at Father, but continuing to stare at her.

"No," she said. "It's you. Your behavior here today is unforgivable. It has confirmed my worst fears. It has knocked me, like St. Augustine, from my horse, and cured me of blindness. Clearly the inordinate amount of time you spend in Granada, or at court in Madrid, leaving us here alone—for which I have been grateful—has damaged your heart. When you freed yourself from the seminary, when you took care of your mother's estate in Carmona, when you came to La Moratalla and met me, when, in your own fashion, and for your own well-known reasons, you courted and proposed to me, you were a better person. Or so it seemed."

– XXXV –

I remained in Sevilla until Carlos departed once again for Madrid.
I made a point of wearing dresses more often. I made it my business to familiarize myself with the Casa de Pilatos, and to ingratiate
myself with the staff. Narciso the coachman was helpful in this
regard. Plans were made for me to visit the Pazo de Oca in Galicia,
and the numerous other properties in Soria and in Leon and
Santander that had become mine as well. Caitríona later revealed to
me that sometime during that ten-day period after Doña Soledad's
funeral, she and Father found time to arrange a series of liaisons that
affected them deeply.

With Carlos gone, Rosario and Francisco, and Father and I, left
for Sanlúcar. Though Father resisted the idea, I pleaded with him
that we stop in Coria del Río. I wished to meet the samurai who had
chosen to stay in Spain instead of returning home with Hasekura
Tsunenaga. Father and Francisco traveled on horseback. Rosario and
I rode in a small open carriage driven by a nephew of Narciso. We
followed the river road and arrived in Coria early in the evening.
Word of our presence spread as soon as Father dismounted—with
his swords and traditional clothing, he looked the way the samurai
who lived there had when they first settled there.

Since then, all six of them had married Spanish women and gradually assimilated. None of their offspring spoke Japanese, and almost
all of the former samurai wore Spanish clothing, albeit of a lowly
sort worn by farmers and fishermen. Only one of them made a point
of maintaining his original identity, a not unhandsome man from
the prefecture of Edo named Akira. We met him the following

morning when he came to our inn in his kimono and *kami-shimo*. Both garments were tattered but clean, and he wore them with a somewhat exaggerated dignity. Wide and thick of build, he had married a shepherd's daughter, who later died without leaving him any children. Like the other samurai, he worked raising sturgeon in the river, harvesting the roe that fetched extravagant prices in Sevilla.

Even though he was older, he treated Father with deference. Much of Father's story—his involvement with the Duke of Medina-Sidonia, his friendship with the former king of Spain, and his passion for my mother—was well known to them. More impressive still, they knew he was the favorite of Date Masamune and considered a prince in Sendai. They both begrudged and, in some fundamental way, respected his refusal to convert to Christianity. What was perhaps uppermost in their minds was that it was he who had recommended this village to them, and who had facilitated their acceptance there.

As the most apt representative, Akira came to pay his respects. Father was cordial with him, but not much more than that. I could sense the man's disappointment. He wanted news from Japan, conversation in his native tongue with a figure of importance, but Father would not oblige him. I did. This man and his comrades were living legends to me, members of the original delegation. Also, with the exception of Father, I had not been with another Japanese person since leaving the Ezochi colony on the west coast of North America. These were men who had grown up faithful to the shogun, men who had followed the warrior's way. Even though they had given that up, they felt far more familiar to me than men like my Uncle Carlos. As far as I was concerned, and especially then when I had only been in Spain for such a short time, they were more like me than anyone else.

The village priest arrived. Father was warmer with this man who wore a dusty black cassock than he was with his former country-man, and after I was introduced, they walked off together toward the village square. I remained with Akira and told him all I could about the homeland, and I asked him about his life, and the lives of the other samurai in that little hamlet. We spoke in Japanese for a good hour.

In the afternoon I went with Father to the spot where, some twenty years earlier, he had been saved—both his hands a mangled mess. He had washed ashore there before dawn one morning after floating down the Guadalquivir throughout the night. The fisher-man who helped him and gave him shelter had passed away, but the man's daughter, Piedad, was there still, married by then to a Spanish man from the village. She greeted us accompanied by two children and a sister-in-law. I could see by the way she and Father spoke to each other that they had been intimate once upon a time. She had clearly been very beautiful when she was younger, but now she had the appearance of someone that years of child-rearing and hard work had taken its toll upon. I made a point of engaging the children and the other woman in conversation, so that Father and she could speak alone, if only for a minute. I watched them walk to the river's edge, and I tried to picture them as they had once been. She was dressed in black, Father in a white kimono with a pattern of dark blue cranes.

Finding myself virtually surrounded by former paramours of my father—Rosario, Piedad, Caitríona—my own romantic yearnings were stirred. I sought out Akira that evening and took a long walk with him. Though nothing of note occurred, I returned to the vil-lage captivated by him. Strolling along the river path, taking into account the way our respective stories entwined, filled me with ten-derness. After I bid him goodnight and entered the inn, Father was angry. He deemed Akira beneath me, and accused his former comrade of trying to take advantage of me, in the hope of getting at my wealth. I found this most unfair and said so, and we fought about it with an intensity that surprised both of us. Francisco was also perturbed by what had been my unchaperoned excursion, and was dismissive of the older man. He and Father's attitudes were a disappointment to me.

Francisco and Father shared a room that night. I could hear them continuing their conversation, regurgitating their mutual criticism of the poor, widowed Akira. Rosario and I slept in the room next door, and to my relief, she understood me.

"You are too close to him," she said, speaking of Father. "The two of you have been breathing the same air for months and years on end. Unwittingly, you've become a couple. And you must realize that you are a magical reincarnation of your mother for him. It is to be expected that he be piqued and jealous at the thought that someone might take you from him. It also makes sense that you would be drawn to an older samurai, a man so like him, at least superficially."

"A samurai of lesser rank," I said. "Having gone through so much to extricate me from the grip of yet another samurai in Sendai," I continued, "one with a very high rank, I suppose it bothers him immensely to see me expressing sympathy for someone like Akira, who committed the great crime in Father's eyes of converting to Catholicism. Despite Father's admiration for the Spaniards and Europeans he has come to know, in their vast majority practicing Catholics to one extent or another, he has never wavered in his view that their dogma reflects a moral weakness, an intellectual embarrassment."

She was quiet after this. I regretted my speech, for I had probably insulted her. We lay there in silence in the dark for a few moments. Some creature, a squirrel or a cat, pawed about atop the thatched roof.

"People need to believe in something," she finally said. "Life is too harsh otherwise."

"I know," I said. "I understand."

***

I woke in the dark, disoriented and disturbed from an unpleasant dream. Once again, I heard a small animal gnawing away at something on the roof. The noise delivered me back to where I was. I looked and saw the figure of Rosario.

"Are you awake?" I asked her.

"Yes," she said.

"Can I come and lie by you?" I asked.

"Of course," she said.

I went to her and she put her arm around me. It was not like it had been with Caitríona at La Moratalla. It was not like she was my sister.

"How did you meet Father?" I asked her.

"I was the lover of the Duke of Medina-Sidonia," she said, "just like my mother had been. He was much older; far older than your Akira. He wished to keep me away from my husband, to keep me in his house. And when your mother arrived with her new husband to visit, the duke made me her handmaiden. Not long after that, your father arrived, and the duke was very taken with him. I believe your father fell in love with your mother the moment he saw her there. After her husband, Julian, left for Sanlúcar, we took a trip to the remains of a Roman village by the sea and stayed a few nights. Your father invited your mother out on a walk one evening—just as you invited Akira. We were all fascinated by him. One morning on the beach he joined a group of fishermen and plunged into the sea prac-tically naked. Your mother pretended to be aloof and refused his advances, and she was displeased when I would sneak out of the tent we shared to spend time with the duke. On one of those nights the duke proposed to me, promising to annul my marriage. It was the last thing I expected. On the way back to Medina-Sidonia, one of his guards, a strong, gruff man who had fought in many battles and thought me still a servant, insulted me. The duke became enraged and challenged the brute to fight, there and then, with his sword drawn. I was terrified I would lose him. Your mother, by simply looking at your father, implored his intervention. He dis-mounted and severed the man's head without a second thought. None of us had ever seen anything like it. We were fascinated and appalled. There was blood everywhere. But the duke's life had been spared. I think, strangely enough, it was then your mother fell in love with him."

This was a story I had not heard before, and I was grateful to her for it.

"But what about you?" I asked.

"In what regard?"

"When did you fall in love with him?"

She laughed.

"What makes you think I ever did?"

"The way you looked at him when we arrived at your house," I said.

"We had all been told he was dead, you and he both. I was over-whelmed to see him again."

"Yes," I said. "I know. But I am referring to other looks that passed between you."

"A long time ago we consoled each other," she said. "That is not the same thing as falling in love."

"What about now," I asked, persisting. "Are you in love with him now?"

"Now it is time to sleep," she said.

But just after she said it she reached out for my hand and kissed it, and I held onto her that night, until the world we live in once again disappeared.

I woke just before dawn. I listened to Rosario's gentle breathing. She smelled good. Out the window was the waning moon. What was left of its visage was sad. Then I remembered it was not a being or a spirit, but a sphere, an orb that went around the Earth, the Earth that was a larger sphere, where everything we did took place, as it whirled through space carrying the oceans and the plains with it.

– XXXVI –

Back in Sanlúcar one thing led to another, and I began to sleep with Francisco. He was insistent that our trysts be predicated on a vow to marry. I concluded that this stipulation was what he required to allow his body to do what it wished, and so I agreed, even though it was the farthest thing from my mind. I was confused, and in need of physical affection. The man I felt the strongest attraction to was married, twice my age, and devoted to a life on the high seas. The older samurai Akira was someone I felt empathy for, but nothing else. Father and Rosario resumed their relationship, consoling each other, as she had called it. He no longer slept in the guest room assigned to him, but crept into the master suite each night where his beloved duke had loved and died. I hid what I was doing from him, and he hid what he was doing from me.

Francisco was young and unblemished and beautiful to contemplate unclothed. As a lover he was coltish and clumsy, selfish and impatient. After our encounters, depending on his mood, he either fretted with religious guilt or became poetic. Accustomed as I was to the simplicity of Japanese love poetry, his baroque Spanish style, employing torrents of words that clashed with each other, was difficult to listen to.

But we got on. It was an agreeable novelty to share my body with someone my own age, someone who was, as the Spanish say, *simpatico*. Despite his occasional eruptions of bluster, there was not a mean bone in his lovely body during those early days. Though I never fell in love with him, I came to love him deeply. I have little doubt the staff and many of the village people soon learned what was going on, and that scabrous and colorful gossip flourished on every street. But the four of us did our best to maintain decorum whenever we were in public, and no one was foolish or bold enough to say anything to our faces.

One of my favorite things to do with Francisco was to ride down the beach to a cove he knew, where we could swim unseen without wearing anything. The pleasure of swimming like that is what I most fondly recall from that month in Sanlúcar. It seems to me one of the sweet advantages of being human—the ability to swim naked with the fish, with the birds flying overhead, to feel oneself as just another sort of animal, and then to retire at night to a comfortable abode close by a fire, dressed and refreshed and fed, and with a book in hand. Each time we went to the cove I thought of how idyllic it must have been for my father and Caitríona when they had their summer together on the island of Paxos. I still hoped Father would end up with Caitríona, for though I came to love and respect Rosario, it was the rebellious, unpredictable Caitríona who held a special place in my heart. It was as if Rosario became a surrogate mother or aunt to me, and Caitríona a sister and friend.

After some three weeks by the sea, Francisco suddenly announced he would be leaving to join a group of friends on a hunting trip. Though I made no effort to stop him, I expressed displeasure at the thought he might find such company and such an activity more stimulating than remaining there with me. He confessed to being too afraid to lose face with his comrades who, if they had to weigh the attractions of hunting against any sort of female companionship, would not hesitate for a second. I told him he would regret it, that if he insisted on leaving, I would return to Coria del Río to visit with Akira. Though I had no intention of doing so, it brought on a confrontation I was sorry for.

***

One afternoon, Caitríona, Carlota, and Inmaculada arrived in the latter's coach. They brought news. In Madrid my uncle Carlos had petitioned the Count-Duke Olivares to help him take possession of the Casa de Pilatos. The count-duke knew the house well, and initially seemed sympathetic with Carlos' notion that such an august residence must only have a family member of the highest ranking representing it. But after considering it further, and perhaps after consulting with the king himself, he told Carlos that the late Soledad Medina was someone greatly esteemed by the royal family, and that her will had been most clearly stated and witnessed, and that the young lady she had left it to, though regrettably lacking certain fine points, was also the only living child of Carlos' departed sister, who had been a great favorite of the former king and queen. Carlos returned to Sevilla furious. He caused such a scene that Inmaculada contemplated leaving the world entirely by retiring to the monastery of Santa Paula. I found it curious that both my grandmothers, despite the vast chasm of space and culture between them, were partial to this form of retirement. In any case, Carlos then took Patrick and headed off to Granada yet again, vowing to never relinquish the boy and to have him enrolled in the king's army as soon as possible. When Father heard this, he took a horse and left for Granada immediately.

According to Patrick, Father arrived in Granada on a winter's day just before nightfall. Hermenegildo and his wife lived in a modest palace located near the Alhambra and the palace of Carlos V. My uncle kept a suite of rooms there. The appearance of a samurai warrior in full regalia, one who spoke perfect Spanish with a Sevillano accent, caused such a commotion in the city below that a procession of the curious followed him up the hill toward the Moorish castle.

Father was made to wait outside in the cold while the trio conspired within. Upon gaining entry, he insisted on speaking with Carlos alone, and they did so in my uncle's sitting room. Patrick managed to sneak outside and position himself by a window where he could hear and observe what transpired within, between the man who had conceived him and the one who had raised him.

"I am here to claim my son," Father said with his customary forthrightness.

"You are fifteen years too late," Carlos replied.

"From a certain perspective that may be," Father conceded, "but seen from another, I have arrived barely in time. Word has reached me of your resolve to 'never relinquish' the boy, and to send him off as a conscript to Flanders."

My uncle kicked a smoldering log in the hearth to bring it aflame.

"My mother exaggerates," he said, "as women are wont to do."

"I am relieved to hear it," Father said, resting his sword and scabbard against a wall. "In that case, you'll place no opposition to my request to keep the boy with me for a time. It can only be good for him, and it will expand his outlook."

"An expansion of outlook is not something we are accustomed to here in Spain," my uncle said. "We've no need for it. The outlook we're born and reared with, aligned with the Holy Roman Apostolic faith, is more than sufficient. It is one the rest of the world should adopt as well. And it is an outlook Patrick adheres to fervently."

According to my brother, Uncle Carlos said these words in a somewhat listless manner, with more melancholy than conviction. Father ignored the small speech entirely.

"You are not opposed, then, to my taking him with me for a while."

"I'd rather you didn't," my uncle replied.

"And you've no plans to put him in the army," Father added.

"In fact, I do," Carlos said. "Military service was the best thing that ever happened to me. It is a necessary rite of passage for a young man, if he is to make his way in *this* world ruled by *our* king."

"Tell me then," Father said. "In what way has your mother exaggerated?"

Carlos, flustered by the logic of the question, became agitated, but again, in a sad or morose way, absent his customary anger.

"Tell me, Shiro, or however you call yourself, what is it you really want?"

"My flesh and blood," Father replied. "I was prevented from being a father to him all these years for reasons beyond my control. But now I can. I am grateful to you, grateful for what you have done for him—for him and his mother. It speaks highly of you. Your sister would have been pleased to know of it. But now, the best thing you can do is to see things clearly. I am the boy's father. I wish to care for him, admit him into my life to the extent he might wish it. I want to provide for his welfare. I am not looking to alter or diminish his faith. I am not looking to speak badly of you, to turn him against you in any way, for you have been good to him up until now, and you are an important figure, a grandee of Spain, a man of influence in what has become his country. But I beseech you not to use him now to get back at me, or to get back at your only sister's daughter for claiming what is rightfully hers, to get back at Caitríona. I beseech you."

My uncle had not expected this, and given the state he was in, with most of his anger gone by then, he was affected by it. The fire crackled in the hearth. Patrick claims my uncle remained quiet and pensive for a few moments, and then said the following.

"When my sister and I were young, children really, we were close. Adolescence was difficult for the both of us. It drove us apart. It drove me into a seminary against my will, and her into marriage with an individual best forgotten. I survived the seminary, but she came to an early death. From what I can tell, her only period of happiness as an adult was thanks to you. And yet I have treated you badly."

"Life is mysterious," Father said, speaking very gently. "It is often brutal and short. None of us asked to be brought into this world. But once here, each of us must do the best we can."

"Talk with Patrick," my uncle said. "See what he prefers. Or no, better yet, just take him with you, for a time, as you say. It should not be his decision. He should not have to feel like he has to choose between us."

"Thank you," was all Father replied.

It was then that he saw, hanging on the wall, so close to the window that for a moment Patrick feared he had been discovered, the red leather quiver with its royal arrows.

"The quiver there," Father said. "It's mine. It was a gift from the former king. I left it at La Moratalla."

"I took it, I'm afraid," Carlos said, "for safekeeping, and for good luck. Take it with you, of course."

Father walked over to it and lifted it off its peg. He smelled the leather. He later told me that holding it, slinging it over his shoulder, brought back many memories. Before they left the room to find Patrick, my uncle said something to Father about a matter that would have terrible repercussions.

"I must warn you," he said. "My companion and host, Don Hermenegildo, is more conservative than I in many respects. He can be vindictive and intransigent in ways I only try to emulate. He has it in for you, for you and my niece, and he will all the more, when he learns how I have capitulated to your request. It was he, frankly, who insisted on Patrick enlisting in the army. The idea came to him, almost in revenge, after Patrick bragged to him about some exploit you apparently had in the Americas, in the settlement of Santa Fe that involved the slaying of some Spanish soldiers. Hermenegildo has looked into it, and discovered that the man who was the governor in charge then, a man of questionable character named Francisco de la Mora, has now returned to Spain. I shall try and steer Hermenegildo off it, but I can't guarantee anything, as his wife is even more determined, and holds great sway over him."

"How is it you have become so close to such a man?" Father asked.

"I'm beginning to wonder," was all that my uncle replied.

All of this made a great impression on my brother. Father and Carlos sought him out and spoke with him, and Father spent the night at a posada so as to avoid having to speak with Hermenegildo and his wife. The next morning, Patrick said goodbye to my uncle and then insisted on showing Father the Alhambra before they set out west. Father had already seen it nineteen years earlier, but pretended he hadn't.

– XXXVII –

While Father and Francisco were away—the one in Granada, the other off hunting—the house in Sanlúcar was inhabited exclusively by women. I was curious to see how Caitríona and Rosario would get along, and was surprised to see how well they did. And it was agreeable for a few days to spend time with Doña Inmaculada and little Carlota. But the concentration of so much femininity soon weighed on me. It reminded me in certain ways of the many days in Japan when I rarely saw anyone except women who were defined by bitterness and regrets. When Doña Inmaculada expressed a wish to return to Sevilla, I jumped at the chance to accompany her.

A few days later, Francisco appeared at the Casa de Pilatos and apologized for having left me so suddenly and in such a manner. I decided to reward him by inviting him to accompany me to La Moratalla, where I was needed to oversee some improvements. It was a place he had heard much about, but had never visited. I asked Narciso to harness his four best horses to the prized coach. As we left Sevilla, an early morning winter mist lay upon the fields. By noon the sun had cleared it, revealing acres of deep green grass and orange groves punctuated here and there with palm trees, and plumes of wispy smoke from farmers burning brush.

I thought of the story Father once told me of his first carriage ride with my mother from Medina-Sidonia to Sevilla. It was at the very beginning of their courtship, when she was still resisting him and even claimed to dislike him. They sat facing each other and now and then, with the roughness of the road, their knees touched. Both

190

of them confessed, months later, that every time it happened, chills went up their spines, the sort of chills I felt when Kurt Vanderhooven touched my skin. I sat facing Francisco for just that reason.

But the road we traveled was smooth and the carriage large, and any chance of physical contact, accidental or otherwise, was made impossible by Francisco's worsening mood. He began to ask me about my love life. The only person I mentioned was Lonan, telling him the very least I could. At first he listened with interest, but the further we went, and the more beautiful the countryside, the more disgruntled his demeanor became. He started to ask very pointed and inappropriate questions, and as I did not answer them, he began to fume with jealousy. None of my explanations, or attempts to put things in proper perspective, made any difference. Eventually I lost patience and said things designed to further wound his *amour-propre*. We entered a cavern of sullen silence, and what had started as a glorious day with a glorious destination was ruined. This was how things were when a rider caught up with us, a messenger from the Casa de Pilatos.

He delivered a letter from Father, from Sanlúcar. It asked me to return to Rosario's house as fast as I could. Short and written in Japanese, it said there was good news, in that Kurt had arrived for a visit, but that there was bad news as well that he would tell me when I got there. I was relieved at being able to call off the journey to La Moratalla. Narciso wished to turn around and return to Sevilla, to head south from there along a well-traveled route. But Francisco, jumping out of the carriage and stalking about like a peacock, insisted we go through the mountains, taking a route he claimed to know from his hunting exploits.

Narciso was concerned that the carriage, more an antique than anything else by then, might not withstand that kind of journey. But we ceded to Francisco's so-called superior knowledge of the area.

It was also a way for me to appease him in some manner. Rather than sit facing him anymore, I sat next to him looking out the window, savoring the views and lost in thought about seeing Kurt again. The letter I had written for him to try to get to Mizuki was back in Sevilla, but I would write another.

The muddy but flat road through the river plains rose into hills where shepherds drove their sheep. By nightfall the hills had grown steeper, the road narrower and treacherous. When the first stars appeared, as Narciso peered into the woods searching for an appropriate place to rest for the night, we hit a large stone, and one of the wheels broke. The carriage lurched to the side. Narciso fell off. We came to a screeching halt. The shock from the sudden cessation of motion, and the whinnying cries of the horses, were only equaled by Narciso's curses that he hurled into the darkness, some of them amazingly inventive and bizarre. One he kept coming back to as Francisco and I made our way out of the carriage was, "*Me cago en dios!*"

With the aid of a lantern we could see that the wheel was shattered beyond repair. Francisco blamed the aging conveyance. I blamed him. Narciso made a heroic effort not to blame anything on anyone, except God himself. We slept fitfully and at the first light of dawn I told Narciso to take a horse for himself and another to follow behind him, and return to Sevilla or to some town nearer by, to try and find help to make repairs. After Francisco insisted that he knew the way, I decided he and I would take the remaining horses and forge on through the mountains. We stripped our luggage of valuables and I asked him for a spare pair of breeches that I changed into. He had never ridden without a saddle and had misgivings, but I assured him he would adjust to it, and off we went. The carriage was left behind in the morning mist, listing and glistening, an enormous jewel abandoned in the middle of nowhere.

Despite his being born within wedlock, being a recognized son of the seventh duke of Medina-Sidonia, being a young and handsome man favored with an inheritance and a title—El Conde de Bolonia—Francisco lived in a state of constant disappointment. It was of course the duke's oldest son from a former union who inherited the grandest titles and properties. But even so, where someone like myself saw opportunities and challenges, Francisco only saw problems. He was that sort of person.

The ride was exhilarating but arduous that first day, climbing steep, bouldery slopes into the Grazalema forest. It was my turn to be annoyed with him, and his turn to do as little as possible to try and improve things between us. He never apologized. We only had food enough to get us through the day. Late in the afternoon I spotted a large hare. Using the only weapon I had, a Japanese knife I always carried with me, and employing the training I'd received and the practice I had acquired crossing North America, I was able to kill the hare from a distance of some twenty meters. I skinned it and gutted it and cooked it for our dinner. Francisco, who fancied himself an expert hunter, was more irritated than grateful. He referred to my knife throw as a "lucky toss." He ate with relish and wanted to sleep with me that night, but I would not have it. This led to another argument and a cold night's sleep.

I awakened to a sword pressed against my neck and the sound of Francisco being beaten with bare fists. Five slovenly brigands were upon us. In a position to take what they wished, they were assaulting Francisco merely for sport and were about to do the same to me before slaying the both of us. Then the oaf looming over me noticed I was a woman. His sword moved the collar of my coat and my strand of pearls was revealed. The announcement caused the other four to pause from raining their blows on poor Francisco. A communal lust rose up in a chorus of cheers, grunts, and vulgar remarks.

Each of them shouted out in revolting attempts to outdo the others for the wittiest and most foul description of what they were going to do to me.

Seeing him distracted with the mirth he was responsible for, I drove my knife through the groin of the man standing over me, deep into his abdomen. As he keeled over screaming, I took his weapon from him. I rose and went at the other four, one by one, until all of them lay dead except for the leader, who was sprawled on the ground in agony. I tended to Francisco's wounds. One of his eyes was shut from swelling. He was doubled over in pain, but nothing had been broken. I retrieved our goods, scattered their weapons, and drove their horses away. Taking a saddle from one of them, I put it on Francisco's horse. Before we left, I put the dying man out of his misery.

Francisco and I spoke very little that day. We traveled well and did not stop to eat, and came down to the sea near the village of Barbate. The route he had chosen placed us a considerable distance from where I needed to go. But we rested there for two days, bathing and eating fresh tuna, so that he might regain his strength. Then we rode slowly up the coast to Sanlúcar. On our final night together, I slept with him as a gesture of farewell. He was rough with me, which I assume he thought was very manly, but quick as usual. I simply let it happen, knowing I would never lie with him again.

When we reached the house and related our adventures, I told our listeners that we had vanquished the brigands between us. Though Francisco was grateful for my lie, he never forgave me for it.

It felt good to be reunited with Father, with my brother, with Rosario, Caitríona, and little Carlota. Upon greeting Kurt, I realized that the waves of girlish flirtation I had aimed hither and thither since arriving in Spain had come to an end. They would be replaced with something else, something as solid and sturdy as his gaze. As he took my hand and kissed it, I was filled with desire, and I prayed the solution I washed myself with each time after having relations with Francisco, just as Yokiko had taught me, had kept me from conceiving.

Then Father took me aside and told me about the charges being brought against him.

– XXXVIII –

I received the following letter from Patrick four years later. The queen referred to in the first sentence, married to the King of France, was the sister of King Philip IV of Spain.

Dearest Soledad-Masako,

Thanks to Queen Anne, which is to say, thanks to you, I have set up house in a small but grand-looking residence near the western tip of the Ile St. Louis. The cumbersome derrière of Notre Dame dominates the view from all my balconies. My work at the embassy is taxing and often dull, but after the midday meal I am free to do as I please and the social life here is amusing.

It has occurred to me, what with the drama that ensued that fateful day, so soon after my arrival with Father in Sanlúcar, that I never had the opportunity to tell you about our journey—one which, given what has happened, I shall never forget.

Before departing Granada, I walked him through the romantic ruins of the Alhambra and the Generalife, two extraordinary buildings, one a massive fort—brutal on the outside, whimsical and delicate within— the other a magical summer palace, both built by the Berbers, who ruled Spain for eight centuries. The gardens were overgrown and families of Gypsies lived in many of the abandoned chambers. Everyone we came across that cold, bright morning was impressed and intimidated by Father's appearance and demeanor, his robes and swords. He cut a rose from one of the thorny thickets, the remaining petals of which I believe he later gave to you.

Then we followed the narrow river Darro into town and I took him into the cathedral to visit the tomb of the Catholic kings. When I told him the tale of how it had been in the nearby village of Santa Fe where these kings had given their permission to Cristoforo Columbo in 1492 for his first voyage, just as they were preparing to besiege Granada and take it back from the Berbers, the irony was not lost on him. The town of Santa Fe the two of you had the misfortune of entering, in the New World that Columbo discovered, was named for the original, just a few kilometers from where Father and I stood that day.

We left the city and rode across a flat, grassy plain. At an inn near the village of Pinos Puente, we stopped for some slices of jamón de Rute, bread, oil, and a glass of wine. We rested for the night at a posada in the town of Loja. There, too, Father's appearance caused a great stir. It occurred to me that perhaps he enjoyed it, being the center of attention, and oftentimes provoking suspicion and antipathy from local people unaccustomed to anything out of their ordinary. The air between us was still tense then, and I asked him about this before we went to sleep that night.

"Would it not be easier," I asked him, "for you to at least dress like a Spaniard, here in Spain?"

"Easier for who?" he replied.

"For everyone," I said. "Though I am mainly thinking of myself."

"I embarrass you," he said.

"Yes," I said. "You embarrass me. My sister no longer wears her Japanese gowns."

"Your sister's situation is distinct from mine. I am a samurai," he said. "Regardless of where I happen to be."

"That means nothing here," I said. "It means nothing to these common people. It means nothing to me."

This last sentence was boorish and unnecessary, but I was still trying to make myself difficult.

"It will someday," was all he replied, before rolling over and pretending to sleep.

I then proceeded to say my prayers, out loud and at a stronger volume than usual, demonstrating thus my continuing allegiance to the Church and, I suppose, to my stepfather.

Then, at dawn, still lying on his back, without any preamble, he said the following while staring at the ceiling.

"I'll tell you other reasons I continue to dress as I do," he said. "I have recently seen the other samurai here in Spain, the ones who stayed behind. With few exceptions they have done what you wish for me to do. But they are lost souls, neither samurai, nor Japanese, nor Spaniards. Their identity has been lost, and some of their dignity with it. I choose to remain a samurai. I am Japanese. This is who I am. You are what you are. The kings whose tomb you showed me in Granada, and the shogun of Japan, made the same mistake. By seeking to conserve the purity of their race through force, they are in dissonance with civilization, *and with nature. Each of us is his own person, to be respected and understood."*

Given the hour, the fact that I was still half asleep, and the cogency of what he was saying, I had little will or inclination to challenge him.

"I'll tell you another reason," he continued, "a personal one. All of the success I have had in this country, with the Duke of Medina-Sidonia, with the former king, with your sister's mother, was because I looked like, and behaved as, a samurai. If I had tried to be like them, to blend in, to dress like them or even worship like them, I would never have inspired any lasting interest."

When he rose in the early morning light I saw his scars for the first time, two gashes about his left shoulder and an appalling series of them along his back. We saddled our horses after a breakfast of bread and Manteca and a strong tea.

"I shall never forget the trip I took, my first exploration of Andalusia," he said. "I traveled through beautiful, untrammeled and uninhabited countryside, from Sanlúcar to Medina-Sidonia, to bring a gift to the duke. For three days I rode with a Spanish friend, hunting for food, bathing in streams, at peace with nature, grateful to be back on solid ground after so many months at sea, grateful to be free of my comrades. I would like for us to do something similar now."

And so it began, five days of living in the wild. On the few occasions I had gone with my stepfather and Hermenegildo on hunting expeditions, there had been tents and servants, cooks and stable boys along. With Father, I never set foot in another village or saw a farm. We remained in the Sierra Morena. Sometimes we could see the Mediterranean shimmering below for hours at a time. Sometimes we rode through dense pine forests. Sometimes we crossed grassy plains and rushing rivers. Father hunted boar and deer, birds and fish. He treated the animals he killed with solemnity. There were no Spanish jokes, or dripping organs thrust at me as Hermenegildo used to do. Father taught me how to shoot an arrow more or less where I wished for it to go. He taught me the rudimentary moves connected with how to fight with his sword.

He described the swords Spaniards used as "pointed clubs." As you know, his katana was sharp like a razor. He told me you were good with one. We swam together, shaved together, we talked about women and nature and about you and my mother. I did not bother him anymore about religion. I said my prayers in silence, shivering under my blanket, looking up at the stars. He said no more to me about his river gods or what he had once called the Spirit of the Earth. He taught me Japanese expressions, curses, the words samurai use to describe erotic parts of the body. He asked me my opinion of the king, the Count-Duke Olivares, the paintings of Diego Velásquez, about life at court. I knew very little about any of those things, but no one had ever asked me what I thought about anything. He actually listened to me. His questions were real. They were not excuses for him to then expound upon his own views. The closest he came to that was when he declared—it was our final night together—that with few exceptions, he thought that misery was other people. He seduced me. He knew what he was doing. And it worked. We came to love each other. A burden lifted from my soul, one I had carried all the years of my still young life, without knowing it was there.

When we reached Rosario's house, he was unhappy about your absence, and yet pleased, proud I would say, that you were doing as you wished. Then Kurt Vanderhooven arrived and you were sent for, and by the time you got there with Francisco, the die I fear had been cast. He never once reprimanded me for having told Hermenegildo the tale of what had happened to you both in Santa Fe, in North America. On the night before you arrived, he had a long talk with Kurt behind closed doors. And now we know why.

His shooting bow from Okayama, and the "le Titien"-inspired red leather quiver with its remaining royal arrows, hang in my bedroom here. Whenever I manage to lure a lady to my abode, she inevitably inquires about their provenance, what they are or represent, and just as inevitably I respond, "C'est une longue histoire."

I trust you are pleasantly settled in Venice. It is my fervent hope we might find a way to see each other, here or there, before year's end.

Your devoted "frère,"
Patricio

– XXXIX –

Soldiers came with a warrant to the Casa de Pilatos, looking for Father. The staff pleaded ignorance as to his whereabouts. Narciso's nephew fled the house on horseback, riding to Sanlúcar with the news. Then a letter arrived at Rosario's, brought by another messenger. It was from Uncle Carlos. He explained that what he had feared might happen had happened, and that he had broken his "friendship" with Hermenegildo because of it. He apologized and offered whatever services he could, and said he was on his way to Madrid to see if he might find a way to intercede on Father's behalf. He also made it clear that, after a violent argument with Hermenegildo, my name had been omitted from the official complaint filed by Francisco de la Mora. It was the one gesture the Granadino made, against the will of his harridan wife, to keep members of Carlos' family out of it. Father was being accused of escaping confinement in the American settlement of Santa Fe, and of murdering eight soldiers in service to the king of Spain. The warrant was for his arrest, detention, and subsequent public execution.

"You must both come with me," Kurt said to us. "I will take you anywhere: Italy, France, England, back to Amsterdam."

Kurt was slimmer and stronger than I remembered him. The broken nose, his sea captain's uniform, his blond hair pulled back and mixed with gray, his piercing blue eyes. To speak the truth, I confess that I was in favor of his suggestion. Despite my great inheritance and the portion of my mother's blood flowing through me, I had not been in Spain all that long, and the idea of leaving it accompanied by Kurt Vanderhooven whetted my appetite. But Father was adamant.

"No. Thank you, but no," he said. "I have traveled too far, sacrificed too much, and beaten too many formidable odds to bring my daughter back here and settle her. To flee would be an act of cowardice. I shall appeal to the king instead. He does not know me, and is certainly under no obligation to receive me, but I will write a letter and enclose the letter I conserve from his father, and I will send Patrick to try and deliver it. Surely Carlos can help with that."

He confessed to me later that even as he spoke these words, he recalled how he himself had tried to deliver the letter from the Dutchman to the emperor in Kyoto, without any luck at all. Fifteen-year-old Patrick left with Narciso's nephew early the following morning, heading straight for Madrid. Kurt made plans to leave us as well—given his nationality, he was still an enemy of Spain in those days. But he invited us to dine with him on his ship the night before he set sail. Father declined but encouraged me to go anyway.

It was the same ship we sailed from New Amsterdam to Europe. It was as clean and gleaming as ever. Its many furled sails were white as snow. As I made my way on board in the late afternoon light, I noticed the low stucco house across the way, where Father and I had first gone, where the talkative Dolores lived with her hens and geraniums. I handed Kurt the rewritten letter for Mizuki. I asked after his wife and family in Amsterdam. He told me of his recent travels.

He served me freshly killed lamb, rice, and wine from Bordeaux, and afterward I let him lead me to his stateroom, where he undressed me in the dark. He removed everything save for the strand of pearls and my bracelets. He kissed me, slowly, and lay me down upon his bed, and then undressed himself. Moonlight entered through the open window, and the ship swayed and creaked against the pilings of the wharf. His passion defiled me, yet his tenderness protected me. It was a revelation. I had found my man. Later, when I returned to Rosario's, I decided against washing myself with Yokiko's solution.

On the following day Father and I said goodbye to Rosario and Francisco. Father thought it best that we go to La Moratalla. Rosario wanted to come with us, but Father discouraged it. She cried and he held her. Francisco, whose eye was still black and blue, stared at them, and then at me. Caitríona and Carlota were to accompany us as far as Carmona. But after we reached the *finca* there and rested for a night, Caitríona insisted on staying with us. I was glad to have her company. We reached La Moratalla that evening. The aroma of budding orange and lemon blossoms filled the cold, damp air and blended with the stoic scent of boxwood.

The staff was surprised, but pleased to see us. Candles and fires were lit. The thought of troops arriving there to arrest Father seemed unlikely and absurd. Carlota slept with me. Caitríona slept with Father. I pined, in a pleasant way, for Kurt, and wondered if Father and Rosario had parted ways. The enormous house and its vast grounds where I was born felt welcoming and safe. I slept as always with the window open. Carlota was curled under the sheets against me deep in slumber, smelling of lavender soap. Just before I myself drifted off, I heard Caitríona in the chamber above us, moaning with pleasure.

***

Patrick arrived in Madrid three days after leaving Sanlúcar. He found Uncle Carlos and showed him Father's letters, and the next day they brought them to the audience Carlos had arranged with the

Count-Duke Olivares. The count-duke stated he knew nothing about the matter, and sent word to the general in charge of crimes against the military. As the two men waited, they exchanged pleasantries as if little were at stake. The count-duke asked about Sevilla, and complained that he had not been able to visit his hometown for some years owing to his great responsibilities. He then took notice of Patrick, his correct clothing, his Asian features, the crucifix he wore around his neck, and he asked him many questions and took a liking to him. The general came to the chamber and confirmed the validity of the warrant that had been issued for Father's arrest. Then, as luck would have it and to everyone's surprise, the king himself entered the room, a fortunate coincidence that in the end altered nothing.

He had been looking for Olivares to discuss another matter, but upon finding such a queer quartet huddled there, and overhearing the general pronounce the phrase "warrant for his arrest," he took an interest. By all accounts, he listened to everyone present intensely, including my young brother. Patrick thought him ungainly and awkward physically, but very kingly nonetheless, and it was Patrick who made mention of the letters which the king immediately asked for. He read the first one carefully, and then unfolded the old sheet of parchment his own father had written and emblazoned with his seal, the one that spoke of Philip the Third's great admiration for Father, ordering that he be treated as a personal friend of the king wherever he went.

As Philip the Fourth was reading, the count-duke spoke of the matter at hand. He cited the heinous influence of Hermenegildo, and went on to detail my brother's somewhat complicated origins. Patrick feared the king might not be listening, so absorbed did he seem by Father's correspondence. But upon finishing it he folded both letters, slipped them into his velvet tunic, and said, "We shall pardon the samurai, effective immediately. Draw up a document to that effect for signature within the hour."

"Yes, Your Majesty," the general said and bowed, turned on his heels, and left in a hurry.

"Count-Duke," the king went on. "Invite the gentleman from Japan to see us here in the palace. It is high time we meet this fellow my father was so fond of. And have him bring your niece, Carlos, so that we might all make her acquaintance."

Then he turned to my brother.

"There is no doubt your parentage is unusual, young man, but so is that of some of my friends and relatives. The important thing is that you have been raised within the bosom of the Church, that you have received the sacraments, that you have been raised to be a proper gentleman. You have shown character and courage in coming here as you did. It speaks well of both your fathers, and we are personally indebted to you for bringing these letters into our hands."

Patrick said he was beside himself with joy. Then the king spoke once again to the tall and bulky Olivares. "This vile governor, Francisco de la Mora—have him detained instead. We have already had news of his scandalous conduct. Out of deference to his family we chose to ignore it, but not after this. The man represented the crown in New Spain. He was charged with the task of administering the true faith to the native population, to win them over to our way of life. But he disgraced himself, and the crown, by entering into unfair commerce with them for his own benefit, corrupting them, taxing and imprisoning them. It is an abomination."

Wine was called for, and the count-duke was all a-fluster what with the unexpected proceedings. While they waited for the general to return with the pardon for the king to sign, my Uncle Carlos felt the need to try and explain the evil actions of his former companion, but the king was not receptive.

"Granada is a city of vipers," the king said, "and this Hermenegildo is a Van der Wyden, a descendant of some of the Germans who helped Queen Isabel drive the Moors back where they came from. They were granted titles and properties in Granada for their service. But those that stayed, like this man's family, were soon infected with the city's nasty vapors, its general proclivity for envy, suspicion, and its darkness of spirit. Perhaps it is something in the water, a curse placed upon the *Acequia de Aynadamar* by Boabdil's furious mother before they fled."

The general returned. The king signed the pardon. It was duly stamped and sealed. The invitation to court, drawn up by Olivares himself, was included in the packet.

"Now gather some strong men and swift steeds, go find this man, and deliver these documents to him. Leave tonight in case other troops stationed in Andalusia are already en route to him."

"I should like to go with them, Your Majesty," my brother said.

"Go then, young man. Go and show them the way."

"I will accompany you," Uncle Carlos said. I shall always treasure him for this gesture, regardless of all the bad business we had before.

***

It took them three days to reach us.

– XL –

On the very next morning after we arrived at La Moratalla, soldiers rode through the gates. They were the same ones who
had come calling at the Casa de Pilatos. From my balcony, I watched
Narciso confronting them. Then Caitríona appeared and stood at
his side with Carlota. It was at that moment when Father came into
my room. He was wearing his finest kimono and *kami-shimo*.
His long and short swords were in his sash. "Come with me," was all
he said.

We made our escape by way of the kitchen. I assumed we would
go to the stables, grab two horses, and leave, but instead he led me
out into the formal gardens, walking at so fierce a pace I had to run
to keep up with him. On we went until we neared the untouched
forest, the wild part of the estate. We crossed the narrow wooden
bridge over the little stream and headed up through the ferns and
pine trees. I realized then that he was taking me to my mother's
grave.

I remember thinking, even with all that was happening back at
the house, how beautiful the morning was, how clean and sweet it
was, how vivid the colors. The undergrowth was still damp with
dew. Spring was close at hand. And I remember how good it felt,
despite the danger, to be alone with Father again. That it was just the
two of us, the way it had been when we left Japan together.

We arrived at the grave and stood in front of it in silence. The
trees and the shrubs were still. The river below was quiet. The sun
had just reached the meadow and was shining upon the upper half
of the Roman columns. Father had not been there since day she was

buried. He looked at the grave, at the Biwa tree that had grown from the seeds he'd planted. He held my hand and spoke to me in Japanese.

"I have to leave you," he said.

"What do you mean?"

"I have to go. I must disappear."

"All right," I said, gripped with fear. "But we shall go together."

"No," he said. "Not this time."

I started to cry.

"Patrick and Carlos will get to the king," I said. "The king will understand. At the very least, he will abide by the wishes of his father."

He squeezed my hand, the way he'd done all my life.

"I have thought it through," he said. "The king is young. He owes me nothing. He will not countermand an order issued by his own military, to help someone who killed Spanish soldiers. Regardless of the circumstances. His honor is at stake. I understand it."

"You do not know that," I said.

"I cannot risk it," he answered.

"Then you must take me with you," I said, desperate. "You cannot leave me."

"We have come so far, Masako," he said, speaking gently. "I have succeeded in bringing you here. I have succeeded in bringing the three of us together again this morning. I cannot ask more from this life. This is where you belong, and now I must return to where I belong. Once I am gone, this next part of your life can truly begin. It is the natural way of things."

I knew him. I knew him better than anyone. I knew the way he sounded when his mind was made. For a long time, this was what I most had feared. I could hardly see through my tears. He turned from me and went to his knees and bowed before my mother's tombstone. He did it in that formal, elegant, samurai manner.

"Don't leave me," I pleaded.

"This moment always had to come," he said, still looking at the grave. "Better it come now, of my own choosing."

"I cannot bear it," I said. "Where are you going?"

He rose and looked at me.

"Home," he said.

And then he kissed me, something he rarely did.

"How?" I asked him.

"With Kurt," he said. "He is waiting for me. Narciso has left me a horse down by the river."

"Kurt," I said.

"Kurt is a true friend," he said. "He will take me back to Japan. Then, I suspect, you shall be seeing him again sometime next year."

"But you are wanted there too," I said.

"Yes," he said. "But I have powerful friends there. And I have always followed the warrior's way. Now it is time for me to retire to a monastery. I am a samurai and it is what I am meant to do. Just as you are meant to stay here, where your mother is from."

I shook my head and felt my body trembling. "I cannot bear it."

Then he put his hands on my shoulders.

"Of course you can bear it," he said, gazing directly into my eyes. "You are my daughter. And you shall bear it with pride. You must look after yourself, and look after your brother, and apologize to him for me. And you must live the life you wish."

Then he drew his sword, the sword given to him when he was thirteen in Sendai by Date Masamune.

"Give your long sword to your brother," he said. "This is yours now."

He held it out in front of him with both hands. I took it from him in the same manner, raised it above my head and then lowered it, the way I had seen it done all through my childhood. The way he wished for me to take it from him. But I could not stop crying.

"You may need it," I said.

"No," he said with a smile. "I have all the weapons I require."

He stepped away and looked once more at the grave before returning his gaze to me, as if to fix me clear in his memory.

Then, before I knew it, the man I love more than anyone in this world strode across what remained of the clearing and began to descend. I followed him and stood by the shrubs and watched him make his way down to the river. Through my tears I watched him untether the horse. I saw him mount and ride off. He never looked back.

Afterword

The next time I saw Kurt, he brought me two things: a reply from Mizuki to the letter I sent her, and a gift from Father. I suspect Father never saw his mother again, because her response, just one sentence long, read, "To know you and your father are well frees me of all suffering."

Father's gift was a traditional wedding kimono, white silk with its "horns of jealousy" veil, and a *kaiken* dagger to replace the one given me by Date Tadamune. He also sent a leather pouch containing a lock of his hair. Thanks to the daimyo of the Miyazaki prefecture, Kurt was able to leave the enclave at Hirado and enter Japan. He accompanied Father to the gates of a monastery high upon Mount Sobo, where they said goodbye. They bowed to each other. He told me that Father made him swear to protect me, in every way he could. Kurt said that Father entered the monastery solemn but content.

Rosario died the following year from fever. Francisco still lives at the house in Sanlúcar alone, and continues to hunt with his companions. I hope he will find happiness with someone.

In 1640 a terrible plague afflicted Sevilla, killing thousands of people, including my grandmother, Doña Inmaculada. I buried her next to Don Rodrigo and Mother's first child. Caitríona, Carlota, and I traveled to Madrid with Patrick, where I met the king, who was gracious and commiserative. From there, we reached Barcelona and sailed here, to Venice. We looked for Paolo Sarpi, only to learn he had died soon after he returned home. We found Maria Elena, the pirate captain's mistress, gray and weak, but alive and overjoyed to see us again. Her beautiful home on the Giudecca was almost a ruin. I bought it and paid for its restoration, and before leaving this world she was able to see it as it once had been. I had a stand made for Father's sword, and have placed it within arm's reach by my bed.

Caitríona's two brothers died in quick succession, and she inherited a significant fortune in Ireland derived from the whiskey and slave trade. She uses her wealth to help the poor in and around Galway. We have a rich and copious correspondence. Often, I ask her if she has found a man to love, but she avoids an answer, perhaps out of delicacy for me, and for Father's memory. She claims she is too busy for such things.

Uncle Carlos found a new companion, an Italian priest. They live together discreetly in Rome. They come and stay with me here at least twice a year, and it is a consolation to see him happy at last. Patrick has moved to Paris, where he works with the Spanish ambassador and entertains. Sometimes I wish he would take life more seriously, as Father would have wished, but he is his own man. Carlota has recently gone to live with him. I live in Spain half the year. I attend to all my properties there, and I care for my mother's grave at La Moratalla, where I can relive my final moments with Father.

Otherwise I live alone with my staff here in Venice, where I have good friends. Kurt visits when he can, and last summer left me with child. He swears he will return for the birth, and that he will soon retire, and leave his wife, and spend the rest of his days with me. He says that he yearns to see me by him in my Japanese wedding robes and veil. But we shall have to see about that. I am content with things as they are. For now, Father's gift is safely stowed away, except for the dagger that never leaves my breast.

Williamstown, Paris, and Madrid, 2017–2018